The Bag Lady,
the Boat Bum
and the
West Side King

SAM LEE JACKSON

AMAZON REVIEWS FOR SAM LEE JACKSON'S
THE GIRL AT THE DEEP END OF THE LAKE

This book has great swag. It's like a cool screenplay already

I rarely finish a book any more. I read this in one sitting.

Run—do not walk—to buy this book!

I couldn't put this book down!

Wonderfully developed colorful characters without going overboard with super hero powers.

Great read - humor, action, good stuff! Buy this one!

AMAZON REVIEWS FOR SAM LEE JACKSON'S
*THE LIBRARIAN, HER DAUGHTER AND THE
MAN WHO LOST HIS HEAD*

A wild ride! Takes its story from today's headlines and plops it down in the most unexpected locale.

Sam Lee Jackson has created an exciting series that makes you yearn for more and more of his books.

This is a rollicking good story with considerable depth of character. Impossible to put down.

I find myself wanting this to be a weekly series, I cannot wait for the next Jackson Blackhawk novel!

If you are looking for a fun read, this is your book!

For Carol, my north star

1

The dirty, emaciated, bad smelling bag lady winked at me.

I was sitting on my favorite barstool at El Patron. It was mid-afternoon and there were no customers. Nacho sat across from me reading a newspaper. Jimmy was behind the bar. Blackhawk and Elena were upstairs. She had a show tonight.

The bag lady had slipped through the door into the main saloon. El Patron had three saloons, two of which spun off either side of the wide, long hallway that led from the main entrance to the big double doors of the third saloon. Each had its own dance floor, but this one was by far the largest. This was where Elena performed. Packing them in. Jimmy saw the bag lady and moved toward me to intercept her.

"Ma'am," he said. "If you go back outside and go around to the back, I'll bring you some food."

That's when she winked at me.

With a jolt, I realized it was Detective First Grade Boyce.

Boyce was a mess. Just a mess. Clothes all raggedy, smudges under her eyes. Hair all greasy and uncombed. On top of that hair was a ragged cloth stocking hat. For an instant I thought my eyes were playing tricks. Fastidious Boyce. Looking rode hard and put away wet. There was even a slight, disturbing odor.

I could do nothing but stare. She moved up to me and slipped up on the next barstool. She slid the arms of her dirty jacket up to her elbows and leaned on them. She cocked her head and looked at me. With that damned knowing smile of hers. Her arms had angry little tracks on them. The tracks of an addict.

I guess I was speechless, so she said, "Looking for a good time, sailor?"

I reached a finger and rubbed one of the spots on her arm. It rubbed off.

"Early for Halloween," I said.

Jimmy was confused.

"Ma'am," he said. "If you'll go back outside, I'll get you something to eat."

"I'm not hungry, Jimmy," Boyce said.

Jimmy frowned, then leaned closer, "Oh my God."

Boyce laughed. She looked at Nacho, "How you doin', Nacho?"

He was smiling, "Just fine Ma'am. I like your outfit."

She grinned at him, "Why thanks Nacho. That's the nicest thing you ever said to me."

"Yes Ma'am," he said. "But not the nicest thing I've ever said about you."

Her face lit up, "Always the sweet talker, Nacho. Always the sweet talker."

"Can I get you something?" Jimmy asked, not sure what was going on. Me too.

"No thanks." She looked at me, "I want you to come outside with me."

"What's outside?"

She slid off her stool. She started away, not looking back. I looked at Nacho. He grinned, shook his head and shrugged. I slid off my stool and followed.

Like I wouldn't.

The sun was dropping in the west. The big parking lot was mostly empty. It wouldn't be for long. This part of the world knew Elena and her big Salsa band were playing tonight, and soon the place would be jammed. Across the lot, by the street, was something I recognized. An unmarked police vehicle. I followed Boyce toward it. There were men inside. I recognized one. Captain Mendoza, Phoenix PD. Mendoza was the head of the city of Phoenix's gang division. Or, he had been the last time I saw him. Maybe he was the police king by now.

Mendoza was in the front passenger seat. I didn't recognize the other man, but he had cop written all over him. Boyce moved around to the other side, signaling me to follow. I did. She opened the back door and waved me in. I slid in. She shut the door and moved back around and stood at the curb. Mendoza slid his back against the door and put his left arm up on the seatback, so he could look at me.

"Detective Armstead, why don't you join Detective Boyce outside?"

Armstead looked at him, then turned his head to look back at me. "You sure, Sir?"

Mendoza just looked at him.

Armstead looked hard at me, then slid out and shut the door a little too forcefully.

"Temper, temper," I said.

Mendoza studied me.

"Boyce knows why we're here. Armstead doesn't."

That didn't require a response.

He looked out the window, like he needed something to look at. "How's the foot?" he said.

"Still gone," I said.

He almost smiled, but didn't.

He studied me some more. Making up his mind, I guess. I waited. I knew he would get to it. He did.

"Ever heard of guy name of Cicero Paz?"

That took me aback. "Can't say I have."

"Runs the drug trade out of Maryvale. Controls all the meth, heroin, whatever sales throughout most of west and south metro area. Ruthless son of a bitch. Destroys a lot of lives."

"If not him, someone else. He doesn't make them buy it. Why would I know who he is?"

Now he did smile, "No reason. But, yes, you're right, he's the guy now, and I want to take him down."

I looked out the window. Boyce had started smoking again. I shook my head. "You have the full resource of law enforcement."

"And, the key word is law. Something we have to observe."

I laughed out loud. "You need someone to break the law?"

He shook his head, like he was tired. "Let's not play games. We both know who you are, and what you are capable of doing, and I might add you have taken matters into your own hands more than once."

"Boyce is undercover. You tellin' me that undercover cops never bend, or even break the laws?"

"Not something I would choose," he said. "But, it's more than that."

I didn't say anything.

"I've got Boyce deep under, and Cicero is a psychopath. She's there alone and these are some very bad guys. I can put someone else under, but I don't think I have anyone that could go to the lengths that might be necessary to work their way inside, let alone protect her."

"And, I would?"

"Wouldn't you?"

I looked at him. The son of a bitch.

"You playing that card?"

He didn't say anything.

"You think because she took a bullet for me. You think because we had a relationship. That I'll do this thing for you?"

He still didn't say anything.

I studied him. Like looking at a wall.

I leaned back in the seat. "You think your guy will get himself killed. And, if I get myself killed, nobody knows who I am. Just a dead body in an alley."

"I think you are better trained than my guys," he said.

I looked at him for a long time. He didn't waiver.

"She in danger?"

He glanced outside at Boyce. "Oh, yeah. If Paz found her out, she'd be raven bait in the river bottom."

I looked back out at Boyce. She was standing next to Armstead, her back to me. She flipped her cigarette butt into the parking lot. This irritated the shit out of me. Blackhawk would have to have the cleaners come out and pick it up. Yes, he is that fastidious.

"If there is anyone that can take care of themselves, it's Boyce."

He nodded, "Yes, but I still want someone to watch her back. I won't say, you owe her."

"I do owe her," I said.

In this very parking lot, Boyce had shoved me out of way of an oncoming bullet, and had taken it herself for her efforts.

"Okay," I said. "Tell me specifics?"

He looked at me then ran his window down. "Boyce," he said. She turned to look at us, came around, and opened the back door. She slid in beside me.

"He in?" Boyce asked Mendoza.

Mendoza looked at me, "You in?"

"Tell me about it."

He knew he couldn't push me. He took a moment, then began to talk. "Cicero Paz operates out of the neighborhood he grew up in. He's like a good old fashion Mafia Don. He controls everything on the west and south side. Nobody spits that he doesn't get a piece of it. He controls everyone. And, that's because he does a lot of favors. You own a small business and you're having trouble with a vendor. The trouble goes away. You got gangs chasing away your customers, suddenly the gangs go away. You get in a bind and can't pay the mortgage on your shop. He gives you the money, and he doesn't screw you on the vig."

"Sounds like a regular Robin Hood."

"Yeah, it does, doesn't it?"

"But?"

"But, if he's done you a favor, then you can bet the time will come when you will do him a favor. There is no choice in the matter. You are going to do it. No matter what it is. You accept his help, and he owns you."

I looked at Boyce, "What's your role?"

"I've established as a homeless bag lady on the block by the bar he operates out of. I watch the activity and report it back to Mendoza."

"But not inside?"

"That would be you."

I looked back to Mendoza, "How are we going to do that?"

Mendoza almost smiled, "Boyce says you have a tactical side to you. She says you'll figure a way."

I looked at Boyce.

"Jesus, Boyce. You stink to high heaven."

She grinned and pulled a baggie out of her pocket. I looked at it. It looked nasty.

"Old, raw, chicken skin," she said. "Keeps the bad guys away better than a suit of armor."

This time Mendoza did smile.

2

I parked the new Mustang at the top of the hill and walked down. The new car was a replacement for the one that had been totaled on the back road to Sedona. This one was still Candy Apple Red and a GT. Maybe it was just me, but it drove a little differently. I was still getting used to it.

I went through the security gate that guarded the dock my old houseboat was moored on. After I had lost the foot, and had found myself back in the world with limited cash, it was all I could afford. Tiger Lily, moored at Pier C, Slip 32, Pleasant Harbor Marina on Lake Pleasant, north of Phoenix. Named by the previous owner. I was too lazy to change it. Blackhawk said it fit my Peter Pan persona.

As I reached the boat I could see something was laying on the stern. It was a big dark mass. Then it moved. It was a dog. A big, old, black dog of undetermined breed. I say old because of the gray hairs speckled through its snout. My sliding doors were open. When I stepped on board it didn't get up, but its tail began thumping the deck. I approached cautiously, my closed fist extended for a sniff.

Now it lumbered up and sniffed my hand, then moved to sniff my pant leg. I scratched behind its ear. My hidden alarm was blinking, I reached down and turned it off. I stepped from the bright light into the shadow of the main lounge. The dog lay down on the stern again.

Old Eddie was sitting on my oversized yellow couch, and Pete Dunn was perched on a bar stool. Eddie was a retired Chicago cop who lived and did odd jobs at the marina. Last summer, Eddie had helped me drag the Tiger Lily out of the water for its annual cleaning. We had sweat buckets as we scraped the lake equivalent of barnacles and painted her hull. Pete was a relatively new neighbor. He had been an ex-attorney and television writer, and had bought the Moneypenny and renamed her *Thirteen Episodes*. Which is what he had sold to buy her. They each held a bottle of Pabst Blue Ribbon. The remainder of the six-pack sat on the galley counter.

"Make yourselves at home," I said.

"Thanks," Eddie said. "Have a beer."

"Eddie said it would be okay," Pete said.

"It is," I said. I took a bottle, and ignoring the twist off cap, opened it with the church key that was laying on the counter.

"Who's your friend?" I said, indicating the dog with a tilt of my bottle.

"Oh, that's Diesel," Eddie said.

"Whose is it?"

"Yours, mine, Pete's, whoever," Eddie said. "Showed up one morning, laying on the dock, back of the bar. No collar, no ID. Seemed grateful for a meal."

"I'll bet he was."

"Know a bit what that's like. So, guess he took to me. He sleeps on board with me at night."

"What's Maureen say?" Maureen was the Marina manager.

"Says, as long as I keep him out of the store and bar. She kinda likes old Diesel keeping the gulls off the dock. Less bird shit."

"Good to be useful." I hooked a barstool with my toe and drug it around to the end of the bar. I turned it and sat on it backwards, straddling the seat, with my arms on the back. "So where does Diesel do his business?"

"I pick it up," Eddie smiled. "Plastic bag it, and put it in the dumpster."

"How you been?" I said to Pete.

"Great," he said. "Starting to get bored."

"You said once you were going to write a novel."

"Easy to say it, harder to do. Eddie and I were talking about how you helped his nephew up there in Cottonwood. Saved that girl and everything. Maybe there's a story there. Nobody ever did say what happened out in the desert."

I shook my head. "Last thing I need," I said.

Eddie was smiling. He looked at Pete, "Told you."

Pete nodded, smiling, "Yeah you did."

"Either one of you guys ever hear of a guy named Cicero Paz. Big meth dealer on the west side."

Pete shook his head, "My world is pretty small right here. I only just met you guys."

Eddie was looking at me, "Christ, boy, what you getting yourself into now?"

"I'm not sure," I said.

"As usual," Eddie said.

"Favor for Mendoza," I said.

Eddie shook his head. "Mendoza don't ask for favors."

"He did this time."

Eddie ruefully shook his head. "Oh man, you're in deep shit."

3

I met Boyce at a Starbucks on 19th Avenue. She wasn't wearing her Halloween costume. She had on her police uniform, which meant black slacks, a crisp white blouse, and a black business jacket. Her badge and gun were on her belt. She was clean and fresh, with her dark hair pulled back in a ponytail. She was standing out front when I pulled up. She was holding a Starbucks cup.

She didn't wait for me to get out. She came to the passenger side and slid in. I started to say something, but she said, "Head south, turn west at Dunlap."

I put the car in gear, "Nice to see you, too."

She snapped her seatbelt in place and leaned back. She grinned at me.

"You are just so sensitive. Tell me again what a rough, tough SEAL you were."

I pulled out into traffic, "I was a rough, tough SEAL. But SEALs are kind and polite just like Boy Scouts."

"Right up to the moment they slit your throat."

"But with a good heart."

"There is that." In a few minutes, she said, "Here's Dunlap, turn right."

I followed instructions. We drove in silence for a while. We finally came to a red light.

"Let's go south a while," she said.

I slid into the left turn lane. On the arrow, I turned. I drove a while. Finally, I said, "You do know where we are going?"

"I'm a Detective," she said. "I know everything."

"Good to know," I said.

"Take a right," she said. I made the turn. We had traveled into a neighborhood of strip malls filled with liquor stores, pawn shops and thrift shops. At the end of one of the strip malls was a vacant lot, then a free-standing building with asphalt parking on the front and side. The lot was surrounded by oleander trees. There was an area in the back where the big dumpsters resided. A sign out front proclaimed it was the SanDunes Bar and Grill.

"That's it," she said. "Drive on by."

We went a couple more blocks, "Go around the next block," she said. I did. We came back to the street we had been on, only two blocks from the bar.

"Find a place to park where we aren't conspicuous."

"You realize this is a brand new, red Mustang convertible. That inherently makes it noticeable."

She didn't answer. I maneuvered to the curb behind a pickup truck with a landscape trailer attached. A crew of landscapers was working on one of the properties. They didn't even glance at us. So much for being conspicuous.

We sat, and watched the bar. An occasional customer would pull into the lot and walk in. Each time I would glance at Boyce, but she didn't react. Finally, a black Beemer pulled in and parked in the spot reserved for handicapped parking. A big man, dark with a black ponytail, slid out, stood for a moment looking around then went in.

Boyce leaned forward, "Little Joe," she said.

I smiled, "Little Joe ain't so little."

"Nick name," she said. "He's muscle for Cicero Paz. Thinks he's God's gift to women."

"What's his real name?"

"Joe Cartwright," she said.

I laughed.

She looked at me, "That funny?"

I shook my head, "You don't know who Little Joe Cartwright was?"

"Should I?"

I shook my head again, "No, I don't suppose so."

Boyce flipped the visor down and opened the mirror that has become standard equipment now days. She unleashed her ponytail and shook her hair out. She applied a bright shade of lipstick that made the red of the Mustang pale in comparison.

She studied her handiwork then flipped the visor back up.

"Let's walk from here," she said, opening the door.

"They won't recognize you?"

She unhooked her gun and badge then stepped out onto the street. She leaned down, put the gun and badge on the floorboard under the seat, and then looked in at me, "Do I look like a bag lady?"

I stepped out. The landscapers didn't glance at us.

"We go in together?"

"Yeah, go in have a beer, leave. Just a couple stopping for a quick one."

We walked across the asphalt parking lot, her arm in mine. I held the door and followed her in. It was gloomy inside, no windows. The place smelled like a bar. Musty, beer, and the residue of cigarettes. Phoenix has a no smoking law now, but somebody wasn't paying attention to it. As you walked in, the bar ran the length of the room on your left. There were four booths on the right wall. Where the booths stopped there was a small pool table and behind that an electronic dart board. There were round tables at the back of the room. This was where Paz's people sat. How did I know they were Paz's people? It wasn't rocket science.

We slid up on stools closest to the door. Little Joe had joined two other guys at one of the round tables. They sat at a set up for five. The bartender was setting a long neck Coors in front of Little Joe.

Boyce sat between them and me, but turned toward me so they didn't have a good look at her. The bartender came and set a coaster in front of each of us.

"What'll it be?"

I ordered two draft beers and he turned to get them. I leaned into Boyce, as if engaged in an intimate conversation. I studied the other two men. They looked to be in their mid-forties. They had the hard, worn look of men that had done things they didn't want to tell Mama about. Their clothes were nice, each wearing a sports jacket. One was completely bald with an earring. Looked like Mr. Clean. The other was Oriental. Mr. Clean leaned toward another table to grab a salt shaker and I could tell by the way his jacket fell that he carried a piece on his right hip. The Oriental guy was leaned back in his chair listening to his earplugs. He was very still, his eyes looking into infinity.

"You know them?" I asked Boyce.

She didn't turn, "Bald guy is Peggy Wieszek. Other guy is Wally Chen."

"Peggy?"

"Yeah, Peggy. Don't make the mistake of making fun of it. I was sitting across the street, saw him beat a guy almost to death for making fun of his name."

"Touchy."

"Very. Got a sheet of strong arm stuff a mile long. In and out. Been out a couple of years now. He and Little Joe are the muscle. Little Joe is pretty much Paz's right-hand guy."

"How about Chen?"

"Chen is a shooter. Deadly as a snake, but he has a clean sheet. He's never been convicted of anything. Not jaywalking, nothing."

"Careful."

"Very."

The bartender returned and placed a beer in front of each of us. Boyce just looked at me. I pulled a twenty and handed it to him. He made change, and placed it in front of me. I pushed a buck to the inside ledge of the bar as a tip, leaving the rest on the bar to indicate we may want another. Bars have a certain etiquette. It's a universal thing. He went back down to the other end of the bar.

"Where's Paz?"

"Has an office in back."

"Tell me about him."

"Already told you most."

"Tell me again."

She shrugged, "Came up in South Phoenix. Made his bones on the streets. Dealing, pimping, small time theft, then came under the wing of Manny Munro. Manny had the south and westside meth franchise. Meth became an epidemic, and they started making money hand over fist. Then somewhere along the line, Manny started using his own product. Got addicted, lost control. They found him OD'd, and Paz was the man."

"Accidental OD?"

Boyce looked at me, "Been a long time since guys like these died accidentally."

4

The door opened behind me. I glanced over my shoulder. A man came from the bright outside, his bulk blocking most of the light. He looked like a bright, white bowling ball. He was really round, and not very tall. He wore a white, long sleeved shirt and white linen pants. On top of his round head was an improbable wig. The kind that makes you wonder to yourself, does he even look in the mirror?

He turned, and beckoned to another man who followed him in. This man was young, thin and jittery. He had an improbable Mohawk haircut, colored an awkward shade of blue. He was wearing a MegaDeath tee shirt with the arms hacked off. His shorts rode low on his hips. He had the gaunt look of an addict.

Boyce swung around, her knees pressing into me as she looked at the round man. She turned back with no outward interest. She lifted her glass to cover her mouth, "Vanilla," she said under her breath.

I looked at her.

She didn't look at me. She took a drink, "That's what

they call him," again, under her breath. "He's Paz's man in the west. Avondale, Buckeye, Goodyear, Surprise, up to Sun City. Runs the franchise."

"Sun City?"

"Huge. Old people like their meth and heroin. If he could get opioids he'd make a fortune. Old people eat up opioids."

I watched in the mirror behind the bar as Vanilla and his buddy approached the three men. He leaned down and spoke with Little Joe. His tone was low, his words unintelligible.

"He and Mr. Clean share hairpieces?" I said under my breath.

Boyce grinned, "Don't underestimate them."

"Never," I said. "Worst mistake you can make. Who's the other guy?"

She shrugged. "Never saw him before."

We watched without watching as Little Joe disappeared down the back hallway and through the back door. He was back a moment later and cocked his head toward the hallway. Vanilla followed his buddy to the door, then the guy hesitated. Vanilla shoved him the rest of the way.

Little Joe looked back at us, but we were leaned together in intimate conversation. The bartender floated our way. I finished my beer and signaled him for two more. He turned back to grab them.

Little Joe came back out, closed the door and sat down. He picked up the beer bottle and held it, but he didn't drink. The bartender came back with two new beers. He set them in front of us. He picked up my empty, but Boyce's was still half full. He placed a new coaster under Boyce's new beer. He selected some money from what was laying in front of me. A moment later he was back with the change. Again, I slid a dollar onto the inside ledge. He hadn't picked up the first one.

Boyce took a sip, "How's Elena doing?"

"There are constants in this world, and Elena is one of them. You need to come see her."

"Yeah, I really should. Every time I do though, she just ends up talking about you."

"Me?"

Boyce laughed.

"She wants us to get back together. She can't stand it that you aren't with someone."

"Who says?"

She shifted to look at me, shaking her head with a wry smile. "Yeah, who?"

"Maybe I'm playing the field."

"Yeah, maybe. That's gotta be some kinda field," she said, turning back, placing her elbows on the bar.

"So, you don't know the guy with Vanilla?" I said to change the subject.

Boyce shook her head and took another sip. A hundredth of an ounce of beer disappeared.

"You need to slow down," I said. "Don't guzzle like that."

"Sorry," she said. "It's the lush in me."

The skinny kid came out from the back room, followed by Vanilla. The kid was ashen, the skin on his face pulled tight with fear. They didn't look at Little Joe or the other two, but moved quickly toward us. The kid was so shook up he tripped on one of the barstools and almost fell. Vanilla grabbed his arm and helped him to the door behind us. They went out into the light.

"That didn't go well," Boyce said.

"Let's drink the beer, and get out of here," I said.

Boyce picked up the old beer, and downed the remains in one gulp. Then she picked up the new beer and downed it in three large gulps. She set the glass down, leaned back and waited a second. She shifted her torso, then let a long and generous belch.

"Amazing," I said. "Absolutely amazing. How can I resist those charms?"

5

Blackhawk was in his office. I came in without knocking. He didn't look up from the papers he had in front of him. I went to the mini-fridge and selected a Dos Equis. I opened the freezer compartment for a chilled glass. Beside the glasses was a multi-colored box. I took a glass.

"Popsicles?" I said.

"I like popsicles," he said without looking up. "Especially the cherry ones."

I popped the cap off the bottle with an opener, and carefully poured the beer. I got all the beer in the glass with the foam reaching the very top. I took a sip of foam, and moved to the leather couch. I sat, stretched my legs out, and crossed my ankles. I took another sip of the foam. Blackhawk continued to work with his papers. I waited.

Finally, with a disgruntled grunt he stacked the papers in a neat pile and set them aside. He leaned back. He took his head in his hands and twisted it one way, then the other. There was a noticeable pop each time. He slid the chair back and placed his feet up on the desk.

"Going straight is a hell of a lot of paper work," he said. "What's up?"

The head on the beer had diminished enough for me to take a decent swallow of cold beer. I told him about Boyce, and what Mendoza wanted me to do. He listened without interruption. When I finished he leaned forward and pushed a button on the phone console he had on his desk. A second later Jimmy's voice came on.

"Yeah, boss?"

"Have Nacho come up here," he said. He pushed the button again to disconnect.

We sat comfortably in silence until Nacho came through the door.

"What's up?" he said.

Blackhawk waved at a chair and Nacho sat.

"Cicero Paz?" Blackhawk said.

"What about him?" Nacho noticed my beer. He stood and got himself one. He sat again.

"What do you know about him?"

He gave a slight shrug, "West side guy. Ruthless son of a bitch. Even the street gangs steer clear of him."

"Does he have any enemies?"

"Who don't? Guy like that, that's all he has."

"Rivals?"

"Same thing to him."

"Anyone in particular?"

"Not really. He scares the shit out of most of the punks out there." He took a drink, "Maybe that new young kid."

We waited while Nacho took a drink of beer. Finally,

Blackhawk said, "For Christ sake Nacho, what kid?"

"New kid down south. Works the area below Baseline. He's new and cocky. Been pushing his guys into some of the other territories. Just now started bumping up against Paz."

"What's his name?" I said.

"Bono Pike."

I smiled and shook my head. "We have guys named Cicero Paz, Little Joe, Peggy, Vanilla and a chinaman named Wally. Now Bono Pike? Who makes this stuff up?"

Nacho shrugged, "I don't know. That's their names, maybe somebody…"

"It's a rhetorical question, Nacho," Blackhawk interrupted.

"Oh," Nacho said. "Why are you asking about Paz?"

I told him what Mendoza had asked me to do.

He shook his head, thinking about it. He looked at me, "Those are some bad dudes. Man, you be careful. Especially with that Peggy guy. He's a psycho."

"How do I get close to Paz?" I asked.

"You don't," he said. "Each one of those guys have made their bones with Paz over a long time. You can't just waltz in."

"Maybe you do him a big favor," Blackhawk said.

"What kind of favor?" Nacho said. "It would have to be one hell of a favor."

"Tell me about Bono Pike," I said.

"Don't know much about him. Pretty young guy. Started with the gangs, soon figured out that there was more to be had than petty stuff. So, he lined up some independent meth cookers and put them together and built a market. I know he's ambitious. Probably gonna get him killed. Especially if he pisses Paz off."

"Paz knows about him?"

"Oh yeah, Paz is watching. Wouldn't be surprised if he didn't have somebody in Pike's organization."

"Pike got anyone in Paz's?"

"I doubt it. Like I said, Paz's people been around a while."

I looked at Blackhawk, "Any ideas?"

"Have to be a hell of a favor," he said.

6

"Have to be a hell of a favor," Blackhawk repeated. We had moved downstairs to watch Elena and her big band rehearse. We were setting at the corner of the three-sided bar. The band was doing a sound check. They had played here forever, but Elena was a perfectionist. She always found something to tweak.

"Like what?"

"You be da idea man."

"I seem fresh out."

We sat quietly, watching Elena run her guys through their paces. On the bar in front of me I still had the same beer from upstairs. I really didn't want it. I wanted something stronger, but I knew if I had one, I'd have two, and I had a long drive home.

"You remember that time in Gabon," Blackhawk said, "when Indigo was hurt, and we were stuck. Our ride couldn't come get us because they had one of those MANPADS."

Shoulder launched surface to air missile, like a Stinger.

Put it on your shoulder and take a helicopter out of the sky. Indigo was one of our ten. The only woman. Hard as nails.

"Twisted her ankle bad. Couldn't walk. What made you think of that?"

"Just thinking about you improvising."

I smiled.

"Well, they had the guy with the MANPAD, and two spotters, up on the side of the mountain. Give him a clear shot if anything came swooping into the valley. Actually, it was a smart play on their part."

"Yeah, smart. Then you carried Indigo two miles on your back, so you could come up behind them."

"Well I'd a gone, just myself, but they had a complete open field of fire. I wouldn't have gotten within a hundred yards of them before they cut me down."

"But, not a woman."

"Not a woman that could hardly walk, and was wailing and crying. They had to be wondering where the hell she came from."

"And stupid enough to go to her."

"Yeah, that too. We were kinda hoping they would be stupid."

"So, the two spotters came out, and she took them."

"Like you said, stupid. The man with the MANPAD stood up to see what was going on, and I took him. Two-hundred-yard shot. Damned good shot if I do say so myself."

"No witnesses," he said with a smile.

"Hey, Indigo saw it."

He did an exaggerated look around. "Don't see her," he said.

"But, I do appreciate you finally bringing the ride to come get me."

"I came to get Indigo. I liked her."

I shook my head, "So you think I should bring Paz a woman, and while he's distracted just shoot him from two hundred yards away, just to prove I can do it?"

"Probably already has a woman, or several."

"So, this wasn't really an idea you were having?"

"Nope."

We sat and watched Elena some more. I finally finished my beer and Jimmy looked at me. I shook my head, and slid the bottle to the edge of the bar. He scooped it up and tossed it in the recycle barrel.

Even in rehearsal, Elena got into her performance.

We watched for a while. Girl could entertain. "How'd you meet her, anyway?"

He looked at me, "I came in here for a drink, once. Ended up buying the place. It was a dump."

"She came with the place?"

He laughed.

"Luckily so. Let's say she succumbed to my considerable charms."

"Considerable," I said. He was looking behind me. I turned. Pete Dunn was walking toward us, from across the large dance floor.

"Hoped I was at the right place," Pete said with a grin. He stuck his hand out to Blackhawk, "Hi, I'm Pete Dunn."

"Pete lives a couple boats down from me. He's a friend of mine and Eddie's."

"Any friend of theirs," Blackhawk said, taking the hand. He indicated a stool beside me. "Have a seat." He turned and signaled Jimmy. Jimmy came down and wiped the bar while Pete got settled.

"What'll it be?"

"You have PBR?"

"Coming up," Jimmy said, moving away.

"You are under Eddies influence," I said.

He nodded, "Yeah, I think so. I'd never heard of Pabst Blue Ribbon when I lived in LA."

He looked at Blackhawk, "So you are the famous Blackhawk."

"Infamous," I said.

"Looks like you are straight out of central casting."

I laughed, Blackhawk looked uncomfortable.

"Sorry," Pete said with a smile. "No offense meant."

"None taken," Blackhawk said.

Jimmy set a bottle of PBR and a glass in front of Pete. Pete started to pull his wallet.

"On the house," Blackhawk said.

"Thanks," Pete said.

"What brings you in?" I asked.

"Nothing really. I was nearby, and I've heard you talk about this place, so I thought I'd see it for myself."

"Be it ever so humble," Blackhawk said.

Pete was watching Elena, "Nothing humble about this place."

He turned to me, "How's that thing going, with that guy with the strange name. Paz, was it?" Then he stopped, "Oh, maybe I shouldn't talk about that?"

"It's okay. We were just talking about that."

I signaled Jimmy to bring me a drink. Man of weak character.

"You're a writer." I said. "Write me the scenario where a guy worms his way into a tight knit group of bad guys."

"How bad?"

"Shoot their own mother and take her wedding ring."

"Whoof. That's bad."

Jimmy set a Manhattan in front of me.

"You serious?" Pete said looking from Blackhawk to me.

"I'd be interested too," Blackhawk said.

Pete thought about it. While he thought, we watched Elena.

Finally, he said, "To be realistic, instead of just some comic book story where the good guy comes in and kicks ass and takes names, I would write that it would have to be over a length of time. You say tight knit so they're not going to accept this guy right away."

I nodded.

"I'd make the guy," he continued, "very non-threatening. No macho stuff that would get the hackles up on the other guys. Harmless, get their guard down."

"Like a one-legged bum?" I said.

"That might work."

"Why would they let him in?" Blackhawk said.

"Probably, because he does something for them. Something seemingly spontaneous. Something that shows he is as bad as they are, but he has no ulterior motive. Something that puts them into his debt."

Elena had finished her rehearsal. Blackhawk drained his beer.

"Should have asked him in the first place," Blackhawk said, sliding off the stool to join Elena upstairs.

7

I let my hair and beard grow.

I found an old fashion boarding house about a mile from the SanDunes, and took a room. I paid by the month. The owner, Mrs. Haggerty, was an older widow, in her eighties, living on a small income. Her body had given up on her, but her mind was still sharp. First thing she told me was that she did her own taxes. Second thing was to ask me to follow her to the basement where she needed a box lifted down from the top of a shelf. The basement was packed with stuff. Easiest way to describe it is to just call it *stuff*.

My room was on the second floor, and had a bed, a small dresser with a mirror and a closet. There was a set of stairs in the hallway that led to a private entrance on ground level. In the closet were extra blankets. On the dresser was a small placard indicating that hotplates were not allowed, but a small microwave was permissible. I don't think most guys that would rent this room would even know what a hotplate was. I knew what one was because us boys in the home were allowed to watch the old TV shows. I had seen Barney Fife get in trouble with his landlady for having one.

I shared a bathroom with two others on my floor. One was a night shift worker for the Post Office. I never saw him. The other was an elderly lady that spent her days watching her small television, and her evenings on the porch sipping tea and talking with Mrs. Haggerty. They rocked on old wooden rockers with cushions covered with wildflower prints they had crocheted. They watched the world go by. Her name was Mrs. Eberle. She told me with pride that she was related to a big band singer of the thirties and forties. I think she said his name was Ray. Ray had a brother, she said was famous too.

In my closet, I kept my utility prosthetic under the blankets, and didn't wear any foot. The floors were old and creaky, and I knew they could hear me stomping around. I was just a guy down on his luck.

I began my assault by walking daily, in the afternoon, with the aid of a single crutch, to and from the SanDunes. Establishing a routine. Timing it to reach the bar in late afternoon. I would sit by myself and sip beer.

I had bought a burner phone and gave the number to Blackhawk, Boyce, Mendoza, Eddie and Pete Dunn. I never used it in public. If asked, I used the name Jack Summers. It was one of the fake driver's licenses I had kept in my safe deposit box. I let it be known that I was looking for work. I didn't carry a weapon except for a pocketknife with a four-inch blade.

Occasionally I would see Boyce, as the bag lady, rummaging through dumpsters. She ignored me. By the second week the bartender, Little Joe, Peggy and Wally Chen had gotten used to me. The bartender's name was Frank.

I normally sat on a stool, by the door, so I could lean my crutch against the wall, out of the way. And, it was as far from Little Joe and the others as I could get. The bar had a dual life. There were really bad guys in the back and regular bar people toward the front. As long as you didn't know, or care, what went on behind the closed doors, it was almost just another neighborhood bar. There was a difference between Paz's guys and the neighborhood regulars. An attitude thing, but I'm not sure the regulars noticed. What I noticed was that, even though Paz must have had an army of dealers on the streets, they didn't come in here often. Just this tight knit group.

I had begun to be recognized by the regulars. Today was Wednesday. The weather was warm and dry. As usual. I arrived at my normal time and slid up on my stool. Also, as usual, I took two crumpled bills from my jeans pocket and laid them up on the bar. Frank brought me my Bud Lite.

"Hear of any work?" I said.

"Like I tell you everyday man, if I hear of something I'll tell you," he said, turning back to stocking the coolers.

I shrugged, and took the beer and sipped it. This was pretty much the pattern. I would arrive in late afternoon and the regulars would filter in slowly over the next few hours. Some of them, would come and stay till closing. Most came for a couple of fortifying drinks before they had to go on home. Today, one of them, called herself Bernie, maybe for

Bernadette or Bernadine, came in just behind me. She usually came in a couple times a week, and she was one of those that would stay till close or, at least, she would still be there when I left. She followed me in, looked around then took the stool next to me. She usually sat further down.

Bernie, sometimes would bring a guy in. Usually a different guy, but always a guy that was big with the money. Buying drinks, betting on the pool games. Flashy. She hung on them, rubbing her tits, and laughing large as they bought the drinks.

There was a young cowboy looking kid, a regular, named Butch that somehow had let Bernie lead him to believe that he was special. The rest of us knew better. Everyone in the place knew better. Everyone in the place knew he was barking up the wrong tree. But, she let that dog bark. Somehow, she had managed to keep those dynamics spinning without crashing into one another, until tonight.

Bernie looked around the bar, then sat next to me. We had only been on a nod and smile basis up till now.

"Hey Jack," she said, situating her purse at her feet. "Buy me a drink?"

"Sure," I said. I started digging in my pocket. Frank overheard her and moved down to us.

He held his hand out, "Save your money, Jack," he said. He looked at Bernie and shook his head. "The man doesn't even have a job. I'll give you the first one on the house. But, that's it."

She looked at him with the highest wattage smile she could muster, "Why, thank you Frank," she said. "I'll have a grasshopper."

A high dollar drink. Since she normally drank beer, Frank looked at her, then shook his head. Amused, he moved away.

While Frank mixed the drink, Bernie pulled her purse back up off the floor, and dug out her lipstick and mirror. She applied a heavy swath of bright red on her lips and studied them in the mirror. She smacked her lips and put everything away. Frank brought the drink. Bernie picked it up, and without a look at me, she moved down the bar toward the middle, where she normally sat.

An hour later the place was active. The pool table busy, guys lined up to take turns at the dart board. Little Joe helped out behind the bar. He was no bartender, but he could draw a glass of beer and make change. Bernie had singled out a young, nice looking guy with strong looking arms, and callouses on his hands. She had drawn him away from the booth he shared with his buddies, and had him next to her at the bar. She was all over him. She wasn't a pro, but she had the moves.

I was just thinking about leaving when Butch came in. He stood by the door for a long moment, then slowly moved forward. Unfortunately, the bar stool next to Bernie was empty. He slid up onto it. Bernie had her arm across the other guy's shoulders. The noise level was high and I couldn't hear what Butch said to her, but I could see her response. She didn't remove her arm and she was laughing, almost taunting. Butch said something else, and the other guy leaned around Bernie and said something. Then Bernie said something to Butch. Something with a heavy dose of disdain. The other guy was staring at Butch with his best hard ass look. Bernie said something else to Butch then turned her back. Butch stood stiffly for a long moment, then turn and stalked out of the bar. Bernie and her fellow were laughing. Bernie signaled Frank for two more beers.

I finished my beer, and reached for the crutch just as Butch came back in. He moved up beside me, and I could see he was holding a large, nickel plated revolver down low behind his leg. I could see Wally Chen notice. Wally couldn't see the pistol, but he could see trouble. Chen moved his hand from near the glass of beer he rarely touched, to his lap. Butch started to bring the pistol up.

I had an instantaneous decision to make. I could let Butch shoot the guy, and the guy would be dead. And, Butch would either serve life in prison or go to the chair, because when you go out to your truck and get a pistol to shoot someone, *that* is first degree intent. Or, Wally Chen would shoot Butch, or I could chance blowing my cover and do something.

I did something.

As Wally Chen stood with his pistol already in his hand, I swiveled and moved my left hand to Butch's pistol as it came up. He was cocking it as he lifted it, and I took hold of it with the web between my thumb and forefinger between the hammer and the bullet. I clamped hard and twisted it from his hand. I hit him in the back of his long hair with my crutch. It wasn't hard enough to put him down, but it staggered him. I tossed the pistol behind the bar and luckily it didn't go off. I raised the crutch to protect myself if the boy decided to come after me. He stumbled two steps, then just stood there, his hand on the back of his head, staring at me.

All the air went out of the room. As if it were planned, the song on the jukebox came to an end. Bernie had no idea what was happening and was just turning. Little Joe, who had been behind and at my end of the bar, moved quickly up to us, came around and grabbed Butch by the back of his neck. He slammed him through the door. I slid off my stool and turned toward the door, my crutch in my hand.

"Wait."

I turned. It was Wally Chen. Peggy stood behind him.

Little Joe came back in. Now I had two in front and one in back. Not a good place for me. Everyone, including Bernie and her boy toy, were watching.

"Who the hell are you?" Little Joe said.

I just looked at him.

"Who the hell are you, I asked," he said, more forcefully.

"Frank said not to talk to you guys," I said.

Little Joe looked at Frank, who was now across the bar from me.

Frank said, "Yeah, that's what I told him. I meant, not to bother you."

Little Joe looked at him for a moment, then he looked at me. He began to laugh. "Get him a drink. Anything he wants." He turned and went back to his table.

In a few moments, the noise level came back to normal. Frank brought me a beer and despite wanting to bolt out the door, I nursed it for a long time. When I thought enough time had passed I gathered in my crutch and slid off the stool. As I went out the door, I glanced behind me. Wally Chen was sitting at the back of the room, his back to the wall, his dark eyes locked on me.

8

At the boarding house, after midnight, I put on my foot, snuck down the hallway, as much as you could sneak across old, creaky wooden floors, and went down the stairs to the outside door. Carrying the crutch, I silently went out the back door and headed for the Mustang. I took the crutch just in the off chance someone came into my room and would wonder why I didn't have it with me. The Mustang was six blocks away. Waiting under its canvas cover in the covered lot. I uncovered it, climbed in and drove to the boat. I needed a break.

The LED light to my alarm on the Tiger Lily was still a peaceful green. If someone had stepped on board, it would be blinking red in its little tucked away spot down low where you had to bend to see it. I went aboard and reset it, drank a tall glass of water, and went to bed.

After the best night's sleep I'd had in a while, I showered, grabbed a bagel, and headed for El Patron. Halfway down the Black Canyon my phone alerted me to a text. There weren't many I knew that would be sending a text, so it startled me. I took the next exit and found a place to pull over. I'm one of those that think it's stupid to try to text and drive. You can manage one or the other, not both. It was from Mendoza. 'WHERE ARE YOU?' it read. I texted, 'on my way to El Patron'. It came back, SEE YOU THERE. I speed dialed Blackhawk. He answered, sounding like he'd been up for hours. His voice, like his shirt, never had a wrinkle, "You at the bar?" I asked.

"Yes."

"I'll be there in twenty."

He hung up. Blackhawk's not much for idle chatter.

Jimmy wasn't in yet, so it was Blackhawk making the coffee when I came into the main saloon. I slid up on my stool, and he carried two steaming mugs, setting them on the bar. He sat beside me. The sweet and low and cream were already there.

"What's up?" he said.

I blew on the hot coffee and took a tentative sip, "Mendoza's coming," I said.

Blackhawk was looking past me, "Mendoza's here," he stated.

I turned toward the double doors that were open, exposing the long hallway. Mendoza came toward us wearing an immaculate, dark blue, pin striped suit. The jacket over a crisp white shirt with a maroon tie. He walked like everything else he did, with compact grace. He slid up beside me and nodded at Blackhawk.

"Coffee?" Blackhawk said.

Mendoza nodded, "Black."

Blackhawk slid off of his stool and went for another cup. Mendoza swiveled on the stool and studied me.

"Heard you had some trouble last night."

"How'd you find out?"

He smiled, which was so infrequent it was a little unnerving "I mean, I literally heard it. We have that place bugged."

"You got Paz bugged, why do you need me?"

"We have general bugs in the light fixtures, but we can't get into Paz's office. That's where he does all his business. Why don't you tell me what happened."

So, I told him.

"I'm not so sure I got away with it," I said. "Little Joe bought it, but Wally Chen is a different breed."

"Only way to find out," Mendoza said, sipping the coffee, "is to go back in there."

"Easy for you to say. Is that why you are here? To tell me to go back in?"

"No. Detective Boyce told me you were in there together when Vanilla brought a punk in."

"Yeah, a jitterbug with a blue Mohawk," I said.

"Found him in a Walmart dumpster on the west side. Two to the back of his head. All the blood was in the dumpster, so they made him climb in there before they did him."

"Man, that is cold. Why'd they do it?"

He shrugged. "Any number of reasons. He must have broken one of the rules."

"One way to get the message across," Blackhawk said.

"ME said he died somewhere between six and ten last night. Were you at the SanDunes then?"

I nodded.

"Who else was there?"

"Don't know who was in the back. Peggy, Little Joe and Wally Chen were out front. Guy named Frank is the bartender. Regulars came and went. I'd probably be looking at Vanilla."

"Golly, you think so? That's great advice." Mendoza leaned back slightly, looking at me, "What are you doing here anyway?"

"Recruiting," I said.

"Recruiting?" he said.

"Yeah, recruiting Blackhawk and maybe Nacho."

Now Blackhawk was looking at me. "Do tell."

Mendoza waited.

"I want Blackhawk and Nacho to take a run at Paz."

Blackhawk smiled, "No problem."

My turn to smile, "But I want you to fail."

Blackhawk shook his head slightly, "I never fail."

"Yeah, there is that. But, I want you to fail this time, so I can be the hero."

"You'll be there to save Paz."

"Yeah. You got it."

I could see Mendoza thinking. "Who are they supposed to be, and why do they take a run at Paz?" he said.

"They work for Bono Pike."

Mendoza nodded slowly, "Yeah that might work. How's Paz going to know they come from Pike?"

I finished my coffee, "I'm working on that part."

9

I was sitting with Nacho, in Nacho's Jeep, in a wide parking lot in south Phoenix. The lot was between two large one-story industrial buildings that housed a row of small businesses. The front of the building had nice shrubbery and attractive glass windows on either side of the private entrance for each business. At the back, each business had a regular door next to a roll up door wide enough for truck deliveries.

We had positioned the Jeep in the back row of the lot where we could see down the back-access area of the building. There was a dumpster by each door. Nacho had done the reconnoitering for me, and said the entrance to watch was the third one down. The air was warm, and the roll-up door was up. Occasionally, someone would step out and stand beside the dumpster to smoke.

We'd been there an hour when two men came out. The shorter one had massive biceps and a sleeve of tattoos on each bare arm. He wore a Diamondbacks ball cap. Backwards. The other man was tall and slender. He had thick, gleaming black hair, and was dressed in a bright red silk shirt and dark trousers. His shoes had long pointy toes and were glossy with polish. He put a cigarette in his mouth and the other man lit it.

"The dandy is Bono Pike," Nacho said.

We sat and watched. The two men didn't talk much. When the cigarette was finished, Pike flipped it into the open dumpster.

"Could start a fire like that," Nacho said. I glanced at him. He was serious. The two men disappeared back into the building.

I sat a moment and studied the back. The driving lane behind the building was curbed with a twenty-foot retention area behind it. The retention butted up against a seven-foot block wall. I turned and studied the parking lot.

"Take me around to the front," I said.

Nacho started the engine, and put the Jeep in gear.

"Go slow," I said.

When we got to the street entrance I said, "Pull over here." There were handicapped and reserved parking signs in the first few parking slots.

He pulled over to the side.

I studied the front, looking both ways down the street. There was a bus stop on the street in front of the building. I looked across the street. There were identical buildings there. They also had a parking lot between them.

"Take me back to Blackhawk's, then come back here and park in that lot across the street. I want you to watch the front here. I need to know if Pike uses the front entrance."

Nacho put the Jeep in gear and we rolled out onto the street.

"Why do you want to know that?"

"I want to know what his daily habits are."

"I'm supposed to be working. You'll have to have Blackhawk tell me it's okay."

I nodded, "I'll have Blackhawk tell you."

Blackhawk told him it would be okay.

I took the Mustang back to its parking lot. I carefully covered it and took my foot off. I put it in a plastic grocery sack and using the crutch, worked my way back to the boarding house. It looked as if I'd just came from a store. I went upstairs and lay on the bed and waited for it to be time to go to the bar.

I dozed off. When I awoke, it was dark out. I almost talked myself out of walking to the bar, but I didn't. The traffic was light, and the air was cooling down. My usual stool was empty, so I slid up on it, leaning the crutch against the wall. I lay some bills up on the bar and Frank brought my beer, and left the change. Bernie was halfway down the bar with a new fellow. I watched the room in the mirror. I watched as the guy left his stool to go to the men's room. He left his jacket behind. As soon as he was out of sight, Bernie went through the pockets. When she saw Frank watching her, she straightened the jacket, and placed it back on the stool. Just being helpful.

Tonight, the time seemed to crawl by. Every second on the clock seemed to take ten. Just about when I couldn't take it anymore, Little Joe came up to me.

"The boss wants to see you."

A thrill of warning went up my back.

"What about?"

"He didn't say. Come on" He turned walked to the back, expecting me to follow. I grabbed the crutch and followed.

Peggy was cleaning his fingernails with a pocket knife. He didn't look up as I followed Little Joe into the back room. Wally Chen's inscrutable eyes never left me. On the side of the short hallway was a door to a storeroom, at the end was Paz's closed door. Little Joe rapped on it, then opened it, and went through. I followed.

Cicero Paz was seated behind a large desk. There was a couch on the right wall. On the left wall were two formal looking chairs, one on either side of a table lamp. The walls were bare. Behind Paz was a wall safe. Paz was a short man. A wide man. He wore a tailored suit that appeared to cost more than most cars I have owned. There was a large, flashy ring on the little finger of his right hand. His hair was black and combed straight back. It glistened with some kind of hair oil. He was clean shaven and there was a faint odor of expensive cologne. He was studying some documents. Little Joe moved to the couch and sat. As he moved I could see the outline of a pistol on his right hip. I didn't sit.

After a long moment, Paz set the papers aside and looked up at me. His expression was non-committal. I had no idea why I was here.

I took in the room without appearing to be furtive. I figured he would have a piece in one of the desk drawers. I could see he was right handed by the way he handled the papers which meant the piece was probably in the top right-hand drawer. If the balloon went up, I would launch across the desk, and go for the gun while getting Paz between me and Little Joe. I was figuring that even if Little Joe was fast, he wouldn't shoot if there was a chance of hitting Paz.

"What's your name, again?" Paz said.

"Jack," I said.

"Frank says you are looking for work."

I nodded.

"Frank's a good bartender but he ain't for shit at cleaning, and he bitches if he has to do it. Someone needs to do it. I need a swamper. I'll pay you a dollar over minimum wage. We usually close at one. You can clean after that until you're done. You keep track of your own hours." He leaned back and studied me. "I find you cheating on your hours, I'll feed your other foot to Peggy."

"Thank you, sir," I said. "No need to worry. I don't cheat."

Paz almost smiled, "Everyone cheats."

Little Joe stood, "That it?" he asked Paz.

Paz made a small wave of the hand, and went back to the papers he had been studying.

Little Joe waved me to the door, and I went back out into the bar.

Wally Chen's eyes were on me as soon as I was back out into the main room and never left me till I was back on my stool.

10

It changed my routine. Now I walked to the bar later, usually around nine or ten. I would sit and sip beer until closing. Closing was less than routine. Closing was whenever Frank decided to leave. He never closed if Paz was still there. Once Paz and the boys left, and if Frank felt like it, he would shut it down. It didn't matter how many customers were still there. Okay by me. The bottom line profitability of the place didn't seem to be much of an issue.

Paz kept his office door locked. It would have been no obstacle, but I decided to play it straight. I was told that once a week Paz would have me come into his office to clean, usually as soon as I arrived at the bar. He and Little Joe stood and watched me until I was done. I didn't attempt to talk, and that seemed to be just fine with them.

After a while, I developed a routine. The last thing I did at night was to bag the garbage, and the recycles, and carry them out to the dumpster. The dumpster was at the rear of the building. At the roof line, in the back, on each corner there were flood lights, but neither one had worked since I'd been there. I told Frank, and he said he would get bulbs, but never did. The back was lined with a thick line of oleanders, so it was dark with the only illumination the ambient light from the side parking.

Tonight, with a bag in each hand, and the crutch awkwardly under my arm, I made my way through the door and around the building. I set the garbage down and was raising the lid of the dumpster when a dark figure stepped away from the wall. I dropped the lid with a bang, dropped the bag of bottles with a crash, and took a step backward, raising the crutch for defense.

"Whoa, cowboy," Boyce laughed. "It's just me."

"Jesus, Boyce!"

She was still laughing.

She always has this uncanny ability to irritate me. I had to smile.

"You wouldn't be laughing if I hadn't kept my highly trained instincts in check."

This made her laugh harder. Then I laughed. "Damn girl." Then we were both laughing.

Finally, I said, "What are you doing here?"

"I thought I'd check on you."

She was dressed like the bag lady, and still carried the faint aroma of dead chicken.

"God, you still stink."

She grinned, "Cool, huh?" She stepped back into the shadow. "Paz and his assholes gone?"

"Yeah, they left an hour ago. Just what are we doing here? If these guys are breaking the law, they're doing it someplace else."

"Oh, they're breaking the law."

"Well, it sure as hell isn't in front of me."

"You're not one of them yet, and you are a civilian, so if they did, it probably wouldn't matter. Not legally. Mendoza says it's going to take time."

I shook my head, "Well, hell, I've got nothing else to do."

"Yeah, we counted on that."

I put the bags into the dumpster, "You stay out here all night?"

"No, a patrol car will come by, a couple blocks from here, and pick me up. They take me home."

"They let you in their car smelling like that?"

She laughed, "They don't like it. They bitch every time, but Mendoza says do it, they do it."

"At least you get a shower and some rack time."

"Not much. I'm usually back out here at dawn."

"Have you seen anything at all?"

"I keep track of everyone that goes in or out. Tonight was unusual."

"How so?"

She cocked her head, looking at me. She smiled. She shouldn't do that as the bag lady, it ruined the entire charade.

"Well I could swear that I saw two guys sitting down the street in a rented Ford Camry.

"Two guys?"

"Yeah."

"How'd you know it was rented?"

"Called it in. And, you know what?"

I knew what was coming.

"What?"

"I got closer and they remind me of a couple of guys I know."

I waited.

I out-waited her. She couldn't resist.

"Looked a lot like Blackhawk and Nacho."

"Could be a coincidence."

"Yea, right."

We both heard the crunch of tires as a car pulled into the parking lot. I looked around the corner. It was the Camry.

"You better get out of here," I said.

I watched a flicker of light as a match was lit. Then as that light grew bigger, the match lit the rag that was stuffed into the bottle. In this light I could see Nacho's face. And, to the side of Nacho I could see Blackhawk. He had a red bandanna on his head. Hidee ho Cochise. I had to talk him into this. He thought it undignified. I had explained there was a reason for it, so he begrudgingly agreed to it.

Nacho slung the bottle out of the car window, and a fire ball exploded.

I looked over my shoulder and Boyce was gone. The Ford spun out of the parking lot and roared down the street. As much as a Camry can roar. I took off toward the front, making long strides with my good foot and the crutch. At the front, the smell of gasoline was strong. The flames were all on one side of the door. The cocktail had broken on the asphalt, not the building and was quickly burning itself out. The stucco wasn't catching, just as we had planned. I had left the door propped open. I went through it and grabbed the extinguisher from behind the bar. I took my time going back out. I stood watching the flames. Waiting until there was just the right amount of damage, then pulling the pin on the extinguisher, I knocked the fire down.

I moved away from the building, toward the street, and studied the damage. The fire was out, but there was enough soot and glowing embers to make the damage look bad.

I went back inside and called Frank.

11

I don't know what I expected, but what I got wasn't it. I thought Frank would show up all agitated, but what happened was that Paz and Little Joe showed up, and they weren't agitated at all. They pulled up in the black Chrysler 300 Paz used sometimes, the one with the 5.7 liter engine and eight cylinders, and the eight speed transmission. They got out and stood there. Just glancing at the burn spots on the building, but looking at the street. Up and down the street.

I stood there, standing like the stumblebum barfly I was supposed to be, and they stood there with their hands in their pockets, looking around, like they expected something. As absolutely difficult as it was, I tried to look dumb.

Finally, Paz turned to me.

"Any damage inside?"

"No sir," I said.

"Let's look," he said.

I followed him in, and Little Joe followed me. When I was here I always tried to make the crutch look more awkward than it really was. I banged it against a stool as I placed it against the wall. I hopped to the nearest stool and climbed up.

Paz didn't look around the interior, like I expected. Instead he walked straight back to his office, and unlocked the door. He went in, Little Joe stayed with me. He was the one that looked around. He even stepped back outside to inspect the damage some more. When he came back in, he stood to one side and leaned against the wall, not looking at me. I waited.

A few minutes later Paz came back out. He came toward us.

"Everything okay, boss?" Little Joe said.

Paz nodded.

When he reached me, he finally looked at me. "What's your name again?"

"Jack," I said.

He dug a wad of bills out of his pocket, he peeled off several and handed them to me.

"You did good," he said.

I took the bills and he went by me and out the door. Little Joe followed.

I sat on the stool holding the wad of bills.

After a while I counted it. It was five one hundred dollar bills. I went around the bar and poured a shot of Wild Turkey into a shot glass, and knocked it back.

"Not a bad nights work for a one-footed barfly," I said out loud. I cleaned the glass and put it back.

The next night I started to the bar with my foot.

It was becoming dusk later in the day now. When I stepped out on the porch, Mrs. Haggerty and Mrs. Eberly were still sitting, their empty tea cups beside them.

"Good evening, ladies," I said.

"Good evening, Jack," Mrs. Haggerty said. She glanced down at my foot. "My goodness, young man. You have a foot."

I lifted it and wiggled it. They both smiled.

"I have a job now. I got paid."

"How wonderful," she said. "Where is your job?"

"There's a bar on Dunlap, called the SanDunes. I clean it every night."

Mrs. Eberly looked very disapproving. "Be very careful," she said.

"Yes, ma'am," I said, not sure about what she thought I should be careful of.

"Mr. Eberly was a drinker," she continued. "But I put a stop to that."

"I'm sure you did," I said.

"The road to Hades is lined with whiskey bottles," she said.

"Yes, ma'am." It was hard not to smile. "I think I'm okay, I just swamp the place out every night. You ladies have a good night. It's been a while since I've walked any distance on the foot, so I'm starting a little early tonight."

I stepped down off the porch and Mrs. Eberly said, "You mind what I said, young man."

"Yes ma'am," I said.

When I got to the SanDunes, the place was mostly

empty. The damage to the outside had already been covered up. Little Joe, Wally Chen and Peggy were sitting at the back. As I slid up on my stool, Little Joe nodded at me. I nodded back. Frank brought me a beer.

"Where is everybody?" I said.

"Most of them are at Ray's Place. They're having a dart tournament there tonight."

"Who could resist that? Where's Ray's Place?"

"Down on Northern. You got a foot." It was a statement, not a question

"Yeah. Mr. Paz gave me a tip for putting the fire out, so I got my foot out of the pawn shop."

"Good deal. Yeah, I heard about the fire. You get around okay on that."

I took a drink of the beer, "Have to get used to it again, but yeah, it beats the crutch."

"You can actually pawn something like that?

"You can pawn your grandmother."

Frank took his rag, and needlessly wiped the bar, "I'll bet we'll be closing early tonight. I heard Little Joe say they had someplace to be later."

"Where's that?"

Frank wiped the bar some more, then went down to the other end. A minute later he came back and wiped the same place again. Finally, he looked at me, "It's those kind of questions that will get you in trouble."

"Got it," I said, taking a drink of the beer.

12

I was in Nacho's Jeep, parked across the street from Bono Pike's place. I had an old Nikon D60 on my lap. It was fitted with a 200mm lens. Across the street, at the bus stop, Blackhawk and Nacho were waiting on the bus. Well, not really.

Nacho was dressed pretty much like Nacho was always dressed, but Blackhawk had his red bandanna on his head. He had an open windbreaker over a ribbed tee shirt, and long jean shorts slung low, down to his pubic bone, showing his black boxer undies. According to Nacho, his attire was what rappers and gangbangers favored. Nacho assured him it was so. He still looked too elegant for a gangbanger, but it was close. He hated it.

If we had timed it right, Mr. Pike should be along any minute. He liked to be dropped at the front. I don't know why, but I was glad that he did. Usually he and the tattooed bicep guy, who Nacho said was called Pony Boy, would get out in front while the driver took the car to the back parking. Maybe the coffee pot was in the front. Or, the cocaine.

We weren't disappointed. Pike's twenty-year-old Lincoln Continental turned the corner and came toward us. Twenty years old, but still looking spanky new. Pike obviously was a fan of Lincolns when they still looked like Lincolns.

Blackhawk was leaning against the bus shelter on one side and Nacho was seated on the bench far enough away so they did not appear to be together. Two strangers catching the bus.

Pike's driver pulled to the curb where he always did, and Pike and Pony Boy slid out. Pony Boy first, then Pike. Pony Boy was looking at Blackhawk who was pulling a pack of cigarettes from his windbreaker. Nacho was looking the opposite direction down the street.

Blackhawk shook a cigarette out of the pack. He approached Pony Boy. I was too far away to hear, but I could see him asking Pony Boy for a light. Pony Boy hesitated, and I didn't really care if he gave Blackhawk a light or not. I had the Nikon up and had the shutter on rapid fire. It was clicking away.

Pony Boy took a lighter out of his pocket. Blackhawk leaned in and lit his cigarette. Pike said something, and Pony Boy shrugged and turned to follow his boss to the front door of the building. As soon as they turned, Nacho stood and pulled the Glock he had kept in the small of his back. He kept it at his side and turned to look down the street, the Glock toward me.

As soon as the two men had turned and stepped away from him, Blackhawk put his hand on his hip, sweeping the jacket back to reveal the shoulder holster he was wearing. I clicked away. Now, I had zoomed back so that Pike and Pony Boy were on one side of the frame and Pike's two body guards, Blackhawk and Nacho, were on the other. Each was watching opposite directions of the street like bodyguards would be doing. If, by chance, Pike or Pony Boy had turned to look back, Nacho was out of their sight, behind the bus stop shelter, and Blackhawk had his back to them, as his jacket shielded the pistol under his arm.

They stood like that until Pike and his guy were inside. A few minutes later the bus came and they both got on. I drove to the next stop and picked them up. We drove back to El Patron. Blackhawk insisted on changing clothes in the backseat. I thought it was funny he couldn't wait. He found no humor in it.

Nacho had bought a burner phone. Blackhawk and I intended to go up to his office to sort through the photos I'd taken, choose the right ones and download them onto the burner phone. We didn't make it. As we stepped into the cavernous saloon we saw a handful of Hispanic men with ladders, stringing bunting and colorful streamers around the room.

All three of us stopped.

"What the hell," Nacho said.

"I forgot to tell you, Anita's getting married," Blackhawk said.

"Thank God," I said. Blackhawk smiled.

Nacho laughed, "Shit, Superboy, you just dodged a bullet."

"Elena is hosting the reception here," Blackhawk said.

Elena's voice rang across the room, "Hey, you boys, come here and give me a hand."

She was back by the door that lead to the large storage room. She had on jeans that seemed to be painted on, a white tee shirt that fit her very well, and a red bandanna wrapped around her head.

"Hey, Dude," I said. "She's got your head gear."

Blackhawk looked at me. Disgusted.

We walked around the three-sided bar to her. The storage room was open.

"I need all those folding tables out and set up. Put the folding chairs around them. Wipe them off first."

"How many to a table?" I asked. I should have kept my mouth shut.

Elena turned to look at me. Her eyes were scathing.

"Anita has found a good man," she said. This sounded like she was implying that I wasn't a good man. At least, that was my first thought. "He has a job." Now that was an accusation. She hadn't been happy about my unemployed status for a while. Or, as long as she had known me. She didn't know about my night time janitor work. I decided this wasn't the time to tell her.

"I'm very happy for her," I said. Suppressing smiles, Blackhawk and Nacho hurried by me, and into the storage room.

"You're happy for her," Elena said. I think this was sarcasm, I wasn't sure, but I knew that somehow, I was in trouble. I was confused. But, that was normal. She looked past me, toward Blackhawk, "Set the tables around the room. Put eight chairs per table."

"That will make it crowded," Nacho said.

"Estupido," she said. "Put one on each end, three on the sides. Three and three and two is eight."

Blackhawk had his back turned, but I knew he was laughing.

I hurriedly stepped into the storage room, anxious to get busy. Luckily, something someone was doing caught her eye. "No, no, no," she said loudly. "Not there!" She hurried away.

I looked at Blackhawk, and he was laughing.

I shook my head, "You'd carry me on your back in a fire fight, but Elena gets on a tear and you run like a scalded dog."

Nacho was picking up two tables, one in each hand, "Me too," he said.

13

It was after the fire, and I was wearing my foot, when I realized I was being followed. The guy either wasn't very good, or didn't care if I knew. I had picked him up right away. After all, how hard is it to follow a one footed guy who walks everywhere? He was in a silver SUV and stayed far enough away that I couldn't really make him out. There didn't seem to be any purpose to it. At least, I couldn't think of any.

Walking to the bar meant I turned four corners, depending on which route I chose. I caught him tagging along behind. Five blocks into it I spotted Boyce, and her shopping cart, on the far side of the street, going through a garbage container beside the Circle K. She had on the same filthy sweater, and ratty, full length dress she always had. I crossed over and walked by her. As I drew even, I bent down and adjusted my foot.

"About a block behind me is a silver SUV," I said. "I'm going in here to buy a fountain drink. When it goes by, see if you can tell who it is."

Boyce didn't look at me. She was engrossed in finding supper. "Right," she said.

I went in, got the fountain drink, stopped to read the headlines in the tabloids then came back out.

"Wally Chen," she said as I moved by.

I nodded, and kept walking. Chen. I tried to think of something I might have done to make him suspicious. It couldn't be anything concrete or he would have shot me by now. I walked another block when two blocks ahead of me I saw his SUV parked at the side of the road. He had his foot on the brake, the brake lights bright. Now it was obvious he didn't care if I saw him. Maybe he was doing something else. I sure couldn't think of what it would be. What the hell did he want? A moment later he pulled away from the curb and drove away. We were only three or four blocks from the bar. I stood, thinking about it.

I shifted my pocket knife from my front pocket to the back. Easier to get to in a hurry, and if I had to reach for it, the movement wouldn't be so overt.

I heard a screeching howl behind me. I looked over my shoulder and saw three street punks rousting Boyce. One was blocking her while another was going through her shopping cart. She was screeching at them. I turned and looked for Chen. Nowhere in sight. I started back toward Boyce.

One of the punks shoved her and she abruptly sat down. As she did, she raised a hand, holding it palm out. Toward me. They didn't know what that meant, but I did. It meant to mind my own business. I stopped walking.

Boyce came to her hands and knees, her back to the guy rummaging her cart. She shifted slightly then lashed her foot out, catching the guy on the side of his leg. He screamed and went sideways. He went down, holding his knee. This astounded the other two. They stood transfixed as Boyce came to her feet. She reached into her cart and came up with a short ax handle with a tape wrapped handle. One of the guys reached down to help his buddy, and in one motion she rapped him across the back of the head, then came back and slammed the club onto the third guy's shoulder. He yelped and fell away from her.

They both backed away from her. The guy with the bad knee was trying to stand and get away from her. The guy she'd wrapped on the head must have had a hard head. He lunged at her, she swung at him, but he blocked it with his forearm and got a grip on her coat. He drew his fist back and she kicked him in the shin. That one hurt. He tried clubbing her, but she pulled away and danced back. He leaned down and rubbed his shin. Dumb shit. With his head in the middle of the bullseye, Boyce spun and kicked him in the head, and he went down.

Boyce backed up to the dumpster, holding the club in front of her. She pointed it at the one she had clubbed in the shoulder. He was the least damaged of the trio.

I could hear her voice, "You want some more?"

The guy helped both of his buddies up, "Fuck you, lady."

Eloquent.

They limped away as quickly as they could. I turned and looked all around, looking to see who might have witnessed this. Chen was nowhere in sight, and no one else seemed to have noticed.

I looked back at Boyce, and she was grinning. She blew me a kiss.

14

Tonight, the bar was busy. Really busy. So busy that Frank came down to the end of the bar where I was sitting and asked me to help him. I slid behind the bar and was soon busy refilling beers and pouring shots.

Since Wally Chen had followed me, I was super sensitive, but even though I would still catch him looking at me, nothing seemed out of the norm. Little Joe and Peggy played Gin Rummy with little notice of the din of the crowd. I was never sure about what Paz did in the back room all this time. Busy running his evil empire, I suppose.

I was happy to be behind the bar helping Frank. I got mighty bored sitting on the barstool sipping a beer, trying to make it last. This getting Paz comfortable with me was boring. Things started to lighten up around eleven o'clock. I was drawing a mug of beer for a tall, rangy looking guy when a little girl hiked her way up on the only vacant stool. I say little girl because she was small, and skinny. She was young, but not that young. There was a well-worn look to her. Her hair was cropped shoulder length and hung straight. No frills. She looked like she could use a shampoo. Probably more than that. Probably a whole bath. She had zero fat on her body, and had that smudged out-of-focus look addicts have. I had to lean across the bar to hear her.

She said something, but I couldn't make it out. I cupped a hand behind my ear. "Sloe gin fizz," she said louder.

"Slow gin fizz," I repeated. She nodded.

I nodded, as if I knew what she was talking about. I moved down to Frank. I tapped him on the shoulder. He turned.

"Girl down there wants a slow gin fizz," I said.

He looked down the bar. "That's Reggie. Haven't seen her for a while. You don't know how to make it?" I shook my head. "I'll do it," he said. He reached behind the bar and took down a bottle. He deftly made the drink, then handed it to me.

"How much?"

He smiled, "Reggie will be lucky to have a buck. If she has a buck, take it."

"If she doesn't?"

"Just give her the drink, but no more."

I carried the drink back to the girl and sat it in front of her.

"One dollar," I said.

She looked at me like I had just insulted her. After a moment, she began digging into her pocket. She fished out some coins and laid them on the bar. Pennies, nickels a couple of dimes, a quarter, a rubber band. Total of fifty-three cents. She stopped digging, leaned back and looked at me. All I was going to get. I had to smile as I gathered the change. I put the change in my pocket, took out a dollar and put it in the register. She didn't seem to notice. She sipped her drink to make it last. I got busy and forgot about her.

By midnight the place had pretty well cleared out. Paz and his crew were still there. Next time I thought of Reggie her stool was empty.

"What's Reggie's story?" I asked Frank.

He shrugged, wiping the bar. "Doesn't come in much. When she does, she's usually more strung out than tonight. Lot of people on the street like her. Don't know much about her. She told me once her daddy is rich, but hell, you can't believe any of these people. She's hooked on opioids, like all of them. Went to heroin because it's cheaper, does meth, krokodil, shit like that."

"What's krokodil?"

"Came from Russia. Homemade shit. Make it out of iodine, lighter fluid, industrial cleaning stuff. Bad stuff. Can rot the skin right off your bones."

"Why do they take it?"

"Why is a doper a doper. If they were smart they wouldn't be dopers."

"She get that here?"

He turned and gave me a hard look. "Paz doesn't allow any drugs in this place. She gets it on the street like everyone else."

I didn't push it. I started cleaning up.

About a half hour later a man and Paz came out of Paz's office and walked through the bar. I hadn't even known that

Paz had company. The man was tall with graying hair. He wore a gray suit. It looked expensive. Paz followed him outside. I wished I smoked so I could have an excuse to follow them outside. I knew better than to ask about the guy.

Finally, the last customer left followed by Frank. I finished swamping the bar. I took the trash out and locked up. I started back to the rooming house. Boyce was nowhere in sight. It was late, and the streets were deserted, only the occasional vehicle cruised by. There is something magically empty about big city streets late at night. You walk a little more quickly. There is a sense that somewhere, if someone threw the big switch the streets would immediately fill with people and cars. And noise. Late at night there is no noise. I reached the convenience store where Boyce had been rousted. Or, I should say where Boyce had rousted the punks.

There was one car in the lot, and I could see the clerk behind the counter, looking terminally bored. I moved past. The next street light was a half block away. It was dark. Suddenly I sensed someone was out here with me. I casually looked behind me. I could see nothing. I crossed the street, glancing over my shoulder. Again, nothing. I took the next corner, went down to a row of hedges then moved into the shadows. I backed against the bushes then squatted to make myself a smaller dark shadow.

I heard it. Small footsteps on the sidewalk. A moment later Reggie came around the corner. I waited until she went by me before I stepped out. She jumped five feet.

"Jesus Christ!" she squealed.

"It's just me, Jack," I said.

"You scared the hell out of me."

"Sorry. Why are you following me?"

"Who says I'm following you?"

That didn't require an answer. "What are you doing out here this time of night?"

She shrugged. She avoided looking at me. The distant streetlight softened her features.

"You have a place?" I asked. She still wouldn't look at me. Then she did, and I could tell she was really strung out.

"I'll give you blow job for twenty bucks," she said, the words rushing out of her.

I shook my head.

She took hold of my shirtsleeve. "Come on, Jack, just twenty bucks. Every guy wants a blow job."

"What do you need twenty bucks for?"

This made her mad. "Ain't none of your goddamn business." She stepped into me, trying to rub my crotch. "Come on Jack, just twenty bucks. I know you got it."

I caught her hand and held it away from me. "You need a fix?" I said. "Even if you had the money, where you going to get a fix this time of night?"

"I ain't no doper," she said, mad again.

"You have a place to stay? You have a place to sleep tonight?"

"For forty bucks I'll sleep with you," she said.

I stood for a long moment, looking at her. "What am I going to do with you?" I said.

She stepped into me, putting her arms around me, "Blow

job twenty, sleep with you for forty."

I disengaged her. Her wrists were skinny as sticks. She had that musky odor of the unbathed. "Reggie," I said. "I'm tired, and it's really late. I'm going home." I turned and started walking. She stayed right beside me, about a step behind.

I stopped and barked at her, "Don't follow me. I can't help you." I turned and started walking again. After a few steps, I looked back. She was standing there watching me. I moved on up the block. At the next street, I looked back. She was following me.

By the time I reached the boarding house she had caught up to me and was just a few feet behind. I went around to the back entrance, which had a small porch attached. She followed. I unlocked the door, went through and locked it behind me. I went to my room and sat on the bed. After fifteen minutes, I went back down the stairs and gently opened the door. She was sitting, huddled in a corner, her eyes were large in the faint light. I just looked at her. She looked back.

I shook my head, disgusted at myself. "Come on," I said holding the door open.

She bounded up, through the door and up the stairs two at a time.

She was giggling while I unlocked my room. "Don't get too happy," I said. "I'm going to sleep, so are you, and you get no money. You just sleep."

We went in and I turned on the lamp. She immediately starting inspecting everything I had. I tried to ignore her. I got into the closet and took the extra blanket out. I shoved the pistol way back into the corner, under a box. I spread the cover on the floor.

"You get the bed," I said. "You're gone in the morning. I have to get some sleep." I took one of the pillows and turned off the light. I lay down on the floor, leaving my foot on. I tried to get comfortable.

She jumped on the bed, then peered over the edge at me. "Ain't you going to do me?"

"Go to sleep," I said. "It's late."

The bed creaked as she lay back. I took my foot off, closed my eyes and tried to empty my mind.

"Hey Jack," she said. "Maybe you could loan me twenty bucks?"

"Go to sleep," I said. "We can talk in the morning."

"I ain't ever known a man that didn't want a blow job."

"Now you do. Go to sleep."

I lay in the dark a long time. After a while I heard her breathing deepen. I rolled to my side and went to sleep. I came awake to find her lying next to me, huddled up against my back. She was sound asleep. I went back to sleep.

When I opened my eyes, it was light. Reggie wasn't next to me. I lay listening. I was alone. Crap, she was probably ransacking the house. I sat up and climbed to my feet. I was a little sore from sleeping on the floor. I put my foot on and went to the door, it was unlocked.

I stepped out into the hallway. I could hear something down the hall. I moved toward the bath and then realized I was hearing someone singing.

Reggie.

I went back into my room and lay on the bed. I put my arm over my eyes and waited. I must have dozed, I came awake when the door opened. She came in, her hair still wet. She looked better. I sat up. I unhooked my foot and rubbed my stub.

She started laughing, "Oh my God," she said. "I didn't know you didn't have a foot."

"Now you do," I said.

"You sure say that a lot."

I reattached the foot. "I'm going down to see if Mrs. Haggerty has some breakfast for us."

"What is she, the cook?"

"She owns this place. I rent this room from her."

"You don't even have your own bathroom."

"It's a boarding house. I share the bathroom with two others, which is why I hope you left it clean."

She had wandered over and was exploring the closet.

"You aren't going to find anything in there," I said. "I'll be right back."

I found Mrs. Haggerty in the kitchen. She gave me a disapproving look. I had to smile.

"Good morning, Mrs. Haggerty," I said.

"Good morning, young man," she said avoiding my eyes.

"I have a guest this morning," I said. "Will it be okay if she joins us for breakfast?"

She turned to look at me, a spatula in her hand. "I can't let this be a common occurrence."

"No Ma'am," I said. I felt silly saying it, like trying to

explain a puppy to your parents, "She followed me home last night. It was late. I couldn't leave her on the street."

"An act of charity," she said skeptically.

"Believe it or not."

"And, what about tonight?"

"I have a friend that runs a safe house for young women. I'll see if he can help her."

She turned back to the stove, "The bacon will be ready in a moment."

When I got back to the room Reggie was sitting cross-legged on the bed holding my pistol.

"You had this hidden pretty good," she said.

15

I was born with a lot of quick. I stepped into the room and with my right hand, pointed toward the corner.

"What about those?" I said, looking toward where I was pointing. She turned her head and I took the pistol with my left hand, bending it back and out of her hand. Luckily, she didn't have her finger on the trigger or I might have broken it, or she might have pulled it, and Mrs. Haggerty wouldn't like that.

"Jesus," she yelped.

I put the pistol back in the closet. I crossed my arms and leaned against the wall, studying her. She was skin and bones. The dark smudges under her eyes couldn't be washed away. I could see the tiny bug-bite marks on her arms where she had used the needle. At least her hair was clean. She smelled like soap, instead of the dusky unwashed smell she'd had last night.

She swung her legs off the bed and sat facing away from me. I think this was her pouting. It was wasted, I really wasn't ready to believe any given emotion from her. Addicts, and especially street addicts could instantly use whatever emotion they needed to get what they wanted. And, they mostly wanted the next fix.

I reached over and shut the closet door, "Come on, Mrs. Haggerty has breakfast for us."

She looked at me, "Me too?"

I opened the door and waved her up, "Come on."

She followed me down the stairs.

As we entered the dining room, Mrs. Eberly was seated at the table, eating. She looked up, then stared at Reggie. This put Reggie on the defensive, so she stared defiantly back at the woman. Mrs. Eberly dropped her eyes with a short sniff and began fussing with her food.

I held a chair for Reggie. At first she was puzzled, then she sat giving Mrs. Eberly a smug look. Mrs. Haggerty came in from the kitchen carrying platters of food. I took a seat.

"Reggie," I said. "Our hostess is Mrs. Haggerty." I indicated Mrs. Eberly, "And, this nice lady is one of my fellow boarders, Mrs. Eberly. Ladies, this is Reggie. A new friend of mine."

Mrs. Eberly gave a short nod but didn't look up.

"Welcome Reggie," said Mrs. Haggerty. She arranged the platters on the table next to the large pitcher of syrup. "We have bacon, eggs, and pancakes and toast this morning. I'm afraid the butcher didn't have the sausage I like, so it's just bacon."

"This will be fine, Mrs. Haggerty, isn't that so, Reggie?"

Reggie looked at me, "Delightful," she said.

I took the platter of pancakes and handed them to her.

She forked three onto her plate. Three eggs, four strips of bacon followed. I suppressed a smile. She stood, leaned forward and reached half way across the table for the syrup.

"I could have handed it to you," I said.

"I ain't helpless," she said. She poured syrup over the top of everything on her plate. Mrs. Eberly was watching, wide-eyed.

Mrs. Haggerty came into the room, a carafe in her hand, "Who wants coffee?"

"I'd like some," I said, lifting my cup. She expertly poured it.

"I want a Pepsi," Reggie said around a mouthful of food.

Mrs. Haggerty didn't miss a beat. "Let me look," she said.

A moment later she returned with a can of Coke. "All I have is Coke," she said.

Reggie shrugged, shoveling more into her mouth.

Mrs. Haggerty placed the Coke in front of Reggie then joined us at the table. She looked at me and said, "Coke's are a dollar."

"Put it on my rent," I said.

We ate in silence for a while.

"Reggie, do you have a job?" Mrs. Haggerty asked politely.

Reggie was wiping up the syrup with her finger then sucking it off. "I'm a flight attendant," she said.

"Which airline," I asked benignly.

She looked at me, cocking her head, her eyes narrowing. "Southwest," she said.

"That must be very exciting," Mrs. Haggerty said.

"Oh, I've been all over the world," she said brightly. "I've been to China and Hawaii and Australia. Just about everywhere."

"You must meet a lot of interesting people," Mrs. Eberly said. I couldn't tell if she was being serious, or snarky.

"How about Outer Mongolia," I asked.

She gave me a look, "Yeah, I think I was there once." She turned to look at Mrs. Eberly. "I met one of those Arabian princes."

"What seat was he in?" I asked.

"13C," she said, giving me a look. She looked at Mrs. Eberly, "He gave me a hundred-dollar tip because I was doing such a good job."

"I thought they had their own planes," Mrs. Haggerty said.

Reggie abruptly stood, "I have to go to the bathroom," she said. She left the room, and we could hear her going upstairs.

Mrs. Haggerty and Mrs. Eberly sat looking sweetly at me. I finished my coffee, "I better go see if she's okay." I stood and retreated behind Reggie.

She was in my room, sitting on the bed.

She didn't look at me as I entered, "I don't feel so good," she said. I leaned against the wall and waited.

She finally looked up at me. "Loan me twenty bucks, Jack."

"I'll do better than that," I said.

"You'll give it to me?"

"No, I'm not going to give you any money. I'm going to

introduce you to a friend of mine. He can help you."

She looked at me suspiciously. "What do I have to do?"

"Nothing. You don't have to do anything. Come on, we're going downtown."

"What's downtown?"

"My friend," I said.

I dragged her down the back stairs and walked her to the nearest bus stop.

16

We had to change buses twice and I almost didn't get her on the second one. I took her hand and pulled her up behind me. When we disembarked we were still two blocks from Father Correa's. Father Correa ran a facility he called Safehouse. He sheltered young mothers who would otherwise be on the streets. I had met him a while back when I had been involved in trying to find a young girl who had ran away from home and had been swallowed up in the streets.

Safehouse was a non-descript building with an industrial feel to it. There was a small plaque at the door to identify it, but no windows or other identifying attributes. Father Correa wasn't in his office. The office hadn't changed much. Small and cramped with a grey metal desk, a file cabinet with the perpetual coffee pot on it, and a couple of simple chairs. I parked Reggie in one of the chairs with orders to stay put and went searching for the good Father.

He was in the laundry room, on the floor behind one of the washers, surrounded by an array of tools. He didn't hear me come in. I stood silently, waiting for a moment when I wouldn't startle him. I could see he was putting his considerable weight on a pipe wrench handle, trying to bust a frozen nut loose. The wrench slipped and he barked his knuckle on the pipe.

"Dammit, dammit, dammit," he said putting the offended knuckle into his mouth.

"I didn't think priests were allowed to swear," I said.

He looked up, his face breaking into a wide smile, "Jackson!" He climbed to his feet. "Priests are supposed to be priests, not plumbers." He grabbed me in a huge bear hug. He was a bear of a man. You couldn't tell he was a priest by the way he dressed.

"It's good to see you my friend," he grinned.

"And you," I said.

He wiped his hands on a towel and examined his knuckle. "Is this just a social call, or something more?"

"Yeah, something more. I've got someone in the office I'd like you to meet. Someone who needs help. The kind of help I can't give."

"Let me wash my hands," he said moving to the sink.

"One thing," I said. "My name is Jack Summers."

He washed his hands under the running water then wiped them on the towel again, "Really? Is that your real name, Jack Summers? Not Jackson?"

I laughed, "No. It's Jackson, but I'm Jack to Reggie."

"Reggie is my new friend? I assume Reggie is female, I can't take in a male, be too disruptive."

"Reggie's a girl."

"Tell me Reggie's story."

"She'll break your heart. She's a little scruff of a thing. Living on the street, doing heroin and whatever else she can get her hands on. I think she's turning tricks to get the money. She offered me a blow job for twenty bucks."

He was watching me.

I smiled, "No, I didn't take her up on it."

He chuckled. "No, I wouldn't think so. Not the white knight."

"Some knight. How much heroin does twenty bucks buy?"

He shrugged. "It changes. Most start on opioids, then go to heroin. Believe it or not, heroin is cheaper than opioids. Is she strung out now?"

"Yeah, she's pretty jittery. I'm surprised I got her down here. I figure she has no place to go and no one to go to"

"I've got a room I can put her in," he said. "I can feed her and clean her up, but she'll have to decide to stay, and she'll have to decide to fight her demons. I'll do what I can to help her, but ultimately it's up to her."

"She had a bath this morning at the boarding house," I said.

He cocked his head, "Boarding house?"

"Yeah, I'm staying at a boarding house."

"You don't have the houseboat anymore?"

"No, I still have it. Do me a favor, don't ask me about it and I will come back when I have everything worked out and tell you all about it."

"Tell me what you know about Reggie. Tell me even the

smallest detail. You never know what might help."

So, I told him everything I could recall about Reggie as we went back through the building to the office. I left out the part about Cicero Paz and why I was working at the bar. I just told him how I met her and how she followed me home. How she sat on my porch until I relented and took her in.

When we got to the office it was empty.

"You have any money in here?"

"I'm not that dumb," he said.

"I'll be back," I said and went out the door.

Reggie was a half block down the street. I caught her at the corner. She wasn't fleeing, just walking.

"Hold up," I said. She stopped walking but didn't turn to look at me.

I moved around in front of her so she'd have to look at me.

"You've come this far," I said.

"For what?"

"I want you to meet Father Correa."

"A Father? You trying to give me religion, Jack? What kind of shit is this?"

I took her arm and gently pulled her with me. "Come on, Reggie. Trust me on this. If he can't help, you can just walk away. This isn't jail."

Father Correa was standing outside on the sidewalk.

"Who's that," Reggie said.

"That's Father Correa," I said.

She giggled. "He looks like….like…"

"Friar Tuck, right?"

She looked up at me, "Who?"

I smiled, "Never mind."

Father Correa was beaming at her. He stepped toward her, holding his big bear paws out to her, palm up.

"Hello, my dear," he said. "I'm Father Correa."

She couldn't help herself. She placed her tiny hands in his. He has the uncanny magnetism that just draws you to him. It's kind of irritating, how he's so damned happy all the time.

Holding one hand, he opened the door.

"I'm just so glad you came to visit," he said. He led her inside.

The door shut and I was standing outside. She didn't even look back.

17

I had talked to Blackhawk and Nacho, and we had decided it was time to make our move. I was at the bar. Frank had gotten so used to me that he never said a thing about me getting behind the bar to wipe things down, clean the mirror, or fill the ice bin. It was one of those half-filled nights. Bernie was in, sitting in her usual spot, half-way down the bar. She had her voluminous purse on the stool next to her. More than once the purse had instigated a problem because she wouldn't relinquish the stool to a customer.

I fixed Bernie an extra strong Grasshopper, and set it in front of her, as Frank was busy at the other end.

I winked at her, "On the house," I said conspiratorially.

"Why, aren't you sweet," she said. She immediately drank half of it.

Nacho came in the door.

"Frank taught me how to make it, is it okay?"

"Yeah it's great." She watched Nacho in the mirror as he came to the bar. She literally licked her lips. She moved her purse, sitting it on the bar. "You can sit here," she said to Nacho, giving him the full wattage.

"Why that's mighty nice of you," Nacho said.

"What'll you have?" I asked him.

"Glass of beer and a shot," he said. "Get the lady another of what she's having. In fact, get her a double."

Bernie hitched around giving him all her attention. I pulled the beer, poured the shot and set them in front of Nacho. I pulled a tall glass and filled it almost to the brim with Crème de menthe. Turning my back, I shielded pouring a slug of rum in the drink. I set this on the bar more toward Nacho than Bernie. She leaned into Nacho and lifted her glass.

"Saluda" she said.

Nacho lifted the shot glass and touched hers.

"Saluda", he returned.

He emptied the shot glass then took a drink of beer. He pulled a wad of money from his pocket and peeled off a twenty. He tossed it on the bar, "Keep the change," he said. He pushed the shot glass toward me. "One more of those," he said.

I turned to refill the shot glass. Bernie had leaned into him, pushing the full weight of her breasts against his massive arm.

"Where have you been?" she said, her eyes glassy and bright.

I sat the shot in front of him and moved down the bar and sat on my stool. Bernie was turning on the charm, and Nacho looked like a man eating it up. When Bernie finished her drink, Nacho turned to look at me and I pointed at Frank.

He waved at Frank, holding up his empty shot glass, "Two more of these," he said.

Frank came down and filled then sat the full shot glasses in front of Nacho. Again, Nacho pulled a twenty and shoved it toward him. Frank made the change and set it in front of Nacho. Over the next hour, Nacho repeated this three more times.

Little Joe and Wally Chen had paid close attention to Nacho when he had come in, but now he was in Bernie's clutches they went back to playing cards.

Finally, Bernie slid off her stool and patting Nacho on the arm, headed for the ladies room. She was concentrating on not staggering. I moved behind the bar and down to Nacho. When Frank was turned away, and the other two were engrossed in their cards, I nodded at Nacho.

He pulled the cheap, burner, cellphone from his pocket. We had down-loaded the Bono Pike bus stop photos onto it. He slid it to me and I dropped it into Bernie's purse. Nacho slid off his stool and left. I returned to my stool.

A minute later Bernie returned and looked all around. She turned to me, "Hey, Jack, where did that guy go?"

I shrugged, "He left."

"Well, son-of-a-bitch!" she said. She climbed back up on her stool. She pulled her purse off the bar and placed it on the stool next to her.

I went behind the bar, and went to the other end where Frank was. He looked at me. In a low voice I said, "I don't want to cause trouble, but that guy that was down there with Bernie. He left. He forgot his cellphone, left it on the bar, and Bernie put it in her purse."

"Well, shit," he said. "She knows better than to pull that crap in here." He moved brusquely past me. He reached over the bar and grabbed Bernie's purse.

"What the hell!" she squealed. "What the hell are you doing, Frank?"

He opened it and peered inside. He reached in and pulled two phones out. Hers had a powder blue cover.

Bernie tried to grab the purse, he held it away from her.

"You got two phones, Bernie?"

She was bewildered. "No, I ain't got two phones."

"Which one is yours?"

She pointed at the blue one, "That one's mine," she said. "What the hell are you doing?"

He dropped the blue one back into the purse. "Where'd you get this one?" he said, holding up the burner.

"I didn't get it anywhere. I ain't never seen that phone before in my life."

Frank handed her back the purse.

"I catch you stealing from the customers in here, I'll have Peggy have a chat with you."

Bernie's eyes widened. This frightened her.

"I ain't stealin' nothing," she said. She grabbed her purse and headed for the door. "I didn't steal nothin'. Fuck you both!"

Frank looked at me.

"Sorry," I said.

"Nothing to be sorry about. I need to know shit like this." He started looking at the phone. I moved to my stool

We had rigged the phone so no password was necessary. We had cued up the photos so the one that clearly showed Bono Pike with Blackhawk and Nacho looking like bodyguards, was first on the screen.

I watched idly as Frank messed with the phone. Then he stiffened, staring at it. He began swiping the screen with his finger, going from one picture to the next. To make it look authentic, we had loaded it with some of Elena's family photos. We had filled the cues with phony calls. Casino's, liquor stores and such.,

I was looking at my beer when he turned to look at me. He pivoted and went to the table where the guys were playing cards. He showed the phone to Little Joe. Little Joe swiped the photos with his finger. He handed it to Wally Chen who stared at it then said something I couldn't hear. He handed it back to Little Joe and they both stood. They took the phone down the hall to the office. I waited.

A few minutes later Little Joe came back out and came down to me. I looked at him, raising my eyebrows, the picture of innocence.

"Yes sir?" I said.

"The boss wants to talk to you," he said.

I slid off my stool and went back to the office, him right behind.

Paz was behind his desk. The TV on the wall was on but the sound was muted. The suit he wore was shiny. Blackhawk had one like it. I think it was seersucker, or sharkskin or some such. The kind of suit someone with a lot more money than me would wear. As usual his hair was slicked back, every strand in place. He was holding the burner. He handed it to me.

"You say some guy left this in here and Bernie lifted it?"

"Yes sir," I said. I grazed the screen with my thumb to wake it up. It was on the picture I wanted him to see.

"Tell me about him."

I grimaced, "Not much to tell. Came in and Bernie invited him to sit next to her. Usual shit she pulls. He bought her a drink, then they started doing shots."

"What'd he look like," Paz said, watching me.

I looked down at the phone. Using my thumb and forefinger I enlarged the picture to a head shot of Nacho. I handed the phone to Paz.

"Like this," I said.

Paz spent a few moments studying Nacho, then he resized the picture and studied Blackhawk, Pike and Pony Boy. Finally, he looked up at Little Joe.

"What the hell is that fuck doing in here?"

"Checking us out," Wally Chen said.

"Yeah, but why?"

"You think he's getting ready to make a move."

"Hell, I've been giving him his space. I wanted to, I'd squish him like a bug."

"He doesn't have the crew to take us on," Wally Chen said.

Paz suddenly realized that I was still standing there. He nodded at Little Joe.

"Thanks Jack. That'll be it," Little Joe said.

Time for me to go. I went back into the main bar and started cleaning.

18

It was Saturday night. The nights were staying warmer longer so Frank left the front door open. There was a soft northern breeze that occasionally found its way into the bar, muting that dead bar smell with something cleaner.

I had been waiting for several days, biding my time, waiting for the right moment. Finally, Vanilla came in and I figured this was as good a time as any. All of Paz's hierarchy was here. I slipped the phone I'd been using from my back pocket and hit the speed dial number for Blackhawk. I waited until it connected then pushed the number one key three times in rapid succession, and hung up.

They were all in the back office, which usually meant something was up. Nobody playing cards, nobody at the bar. I hoped they would stay there awhile. They did. Almost an hour passed before Little Joe came back out and spoke to Frank. Frank took his apron off and came down to me.

"I'm going with the boss. I need you to tend the bar till I'm back."

"Sure thing," I said. I stepped behind the bar and

wrapped an old apron I had been using around my waist. Frank went to the back. Behind the bar was a small garbage can with a plastic bag liner. It was half full. I went through the bar and put everything trashy I could find in it. I pulled the filled liner from the can and tied it at the top. I put a new bag in, and sat the bag of garbage behind the end of the bar, steps from the door.

The guys were back in the office so long I began to worry that I had misjudged. Maybe they weren't going anywhere. Paz was not a team meeting kind of guy. He dealt one on one. With them all together, I figured they had something planned. I was setting a mug of beer in front of an old grizzled guy with more hair in his ears and nose than on his head when the back-office door opened. I turned and moved closer to the bag of garbage. I got busy wiping things down. They were leaving. Peggy and Vanilla came out first, followed by Wally Chen and Frank. Little Joe preceded Paz. Paz came out adjusting his suit coat like a man adjusting a hidden piece. He was impeccable. They filed through the front door, into the parking lot. As Paz went by me, I picked up the garbage and followed him out. He paused just outside and glanced back. He saw I was taking garbage out. He looked at me a second then stepped out into the parking lot toward the big, black SUV he used. I was right behind him, but not too close. Wally Chen was walking across the lot toward Paz's vehicle. Peggy and Vanilla were lighting a quick smoke before they would get into Paz's car. Never could figure that out. Two puffs and throw it away.

The lot was dimly illuminated by pole lights on either

side. The SanDunes sign lit part of the street. Across the road, a street light lit up the far side and the sidewalk. Timing is everything. Blackhawk was on his.

I was a step behind Paz when an older Lincoln Continental pulled rapidly into the light on the street. It came to a screeching halt. Nacho popped out of the driver's side. Blackhawk came around the front. Blackhawk was sporting his trademark red bandanna, and they both had AK's.

Little Joe yelled, "Boss!" as he ducked and pulled his piece. Blackhawk and Nacho opened fire.

I dropped the bag of garbage at the first shot and slammed into Paz. He was trying to pull his piece as I knocked him off his feet. I threw myself on top of him, pinning his gun hand. Blackhawk's rounds slammed around us spitting dirt and plaster everywhere. Nacho's rounds flew harmlessly into the night sky, but they didn't know that. It lasted just a few seconds then as quickly as it started, Blackhawk and Nacho and the Lincoln roared away.

Peggy and Vanilla had thrown themselves behind Paz's SUV. Wally Chen was on one knee firing at the retreating Lincoln. Little Joe rushed over to us, his pistol in his hand.

The shots were still ringing in my ears. Paz was struggling under me.

"Get the fuck off of me. Get the fuck off of me."

I rolled off and came to my hands and knees.

Paz scrambled to his feet. "Goddammit, what the hell are you doing." He had his pistol out pointing it at my face. "You stupid son-of-a-bitch!"

Little Joe stepped over and took his hand. He gently pulled the muzzle away from me.

"Hold it boss. Hold on, he was trying to help you. He was covering you up."

"Shit," Paz said, jerking his hand away. He started dusting his clothes off. Peggy and Wally Chen were staring at the street where the Lincoln had disappeared. Their guns were ready but they had no one to shoot. Vanilla was getting to his feet, his white suit smudged by the asphalt. Wally Chen began to reload.

"What the hell was that?" Paz demanded.

I waited. I wanted someone else to say it. Little Joe did.

"Those were Bono Pike's guys."

"That was Pike?" Paz said, still trying to get the dirt off his suit.

"One of those guys looked like that guy that came into the bar. The guy that Bernie stole the phone from," I said.

"Yeah," Frank said. "That was the guy, and the guy with the bandanna was in those pictures."

"Fuck," Paz said. "Somebody get me another suit out of the closet." He turned and stared down the street for a long moment, then went back inside. We all followed.

The customers weren't sure what to do. They didn't know whether to duck or run.

"Bar's closed," Frank said loudly. He turned to me, "Close it up."

Paz, followed by his guys, went down the hall to the back. Frank went with them.

I shooed all the customers out. They were reluctant to go outside.

"It's okay," I said loudly. "It's all over. It's safe. Go home."

Finally, there was only old hairy ears left.

"Time to go," I said.

He finished his beer in two gulps. "What the hell are they celebrating out there?"

"Disneyland at night," I said. "Time to go."

I followed him. When he was outside, I closed the door. I spent the next half hour cleaning up. When I finished I wasn't sure whether to leave or not. I decided to wait.

Finally, the back door opened and the guys filed out. Just like before, with Paz taking up the rear. He had a new suit on.

Frank gave me a look I didn't understand. He went past me and opened the door. He held it as the others trooped out. None of them looked at me.

Paz stopped beside me.

"I want you to come with us," he said. He turned without waiting for a response. I followed him out.

19

There were so many of us we took two cars. Little Joe waved me into his black Beemer. I climbed into the front passenger seat. The rest were in Paz's SUV. Little Joe followed Paz's SUV as it pulled out of the parking lot. I thought I caught a glimpse of Boyce, but couldn't be sure. A shadow behind a dumpster. There was hardly any traffic. We followed through the night streets. Little Joe blew through a couple of stoplights keeping up.

We followed Dunlap to where it became Olive and continued west. After a while we ducked south and drove into downtown Old Glendale. Eventually we pulled over and parked on the street. Both drivers had cut their lights as they pulled to the curb.

I expected to be getting out, but we didn't. Little Joe shifted in his seat to get comfortable. I did the same. I looked around. There weren't many people on the street. A half block ahead I could see an occasional car pull to the curb. A man came out of the shadows and a transaction took place. The cars drove away and the man would disappear back into the shadows.

Little Joe was sitting comfortably, watching.

"I hear talk in the bar," I said. Little Joe didn't appear to hear me. "They say that Paz controls all the drug trade on the west side." Little Joe sat silently. He didn't answer. "I'm not in any trouble, am I?"

Finally, Little Joe turned to look at me. "Mr. Paz is the king of the west side. Nothing goes down he doesn't have a piece of."

I didn't say anything.

"You're not in trouble," he continued. "Mr. Paz was impressed with how you reacted when those assholes opened up on us."

He turned to watch another car pull to the curb and the shadow man come out to it.

"Who were those guys that tried to shoot us?"

"Ain't no us. They were after Mr. Paz. You notice how Vanilla dove to the ground as far from Mr. Paz as he could get? They work for a guy name of Bono Pike. He's starting to get big for his britches. He thinks he can take Mr. Paz's business from him."

I watched the shadow man plying his trade. "Is that the Pike guy?"

He laughed. "Hell no. Pike's down in south central. This guy's a greedy little shit who thinks he can skim Mr. Paz's money."

"But, you guys know he's doing it."

"You ask too many questions. Just sit and watch."

After ten minutes of watching, the lights on Paz's SUV came on. Little Joe started his engine. The SUV pulled away from the curb and quickly moved down to where the customers had been pulling to the curb. Little Joe pulled in behind.

"Come on," he said sharply, and piled out of his door. I followed suit.

Everyone was out. The man tried to run but Wally Chen and Frank blocked him. Peggy got a hold of him and slung him against the stucco wall. He practically flew, and his body made an audible thump against the wall. The man slumped to the ground. He was a black guy with a shaven head and earrings. He wasn't small.

He looked around, eyes wide with fright. He scrambled up against the wall. Paz signaled to Frank and Little Joe and they put their hands on him, and lifted him to his feet. All these bad guys around him, but his eyes were locked on Cicero Paz. Paz frightened him.

"Hey man," he stuttered. "I was coming by tomorrow. No shit man, I was gonna bring you the juice."

Paz held his hand out, palm up.

The man didn't hesitate. He pulled a zippered pouch out of his back pocket and handed it to Paz. Paz unzipped it and pulled a thick stack of bills out.

"I'm told you are keeping more than the appropriate amount for yourself," Paz said. He carefully enunciated each syllable in *appropriate*.

The man was shaking his head. "Uh, nope, I ain't done that."

"So, you are saying that the man that told me that is lying?"

"Oh, yeah Mr. Paz. Whoever told you that is lying. I know better than to try to cheat you."

"So, I want to be sure. Whoever told me that, was lying?"

"Yessir."

Paz turned to Peggy, "The man says you are lying, Peggy."

This terrified the man. He slumped down again. He began to whimper.

"No one calls me a liar and lives," Peggy said. He pulled his hand gun from his belt and pointed it at the man's head. It was a Colt 45acp 1911 semi-automatic. All the whimpering man could do was to hold up a hand, palm out, to ward off the bullet.

"Have Jack shoot him," Wally Chen said.

Peggy lowered his gun, "That's a good idea." He reversed the gun and thrust it at me.

I looked at the gun, then at him, revealing nothing.

"What's the matter, you don't have the balls?"

"Way above my pay grade," I said.

"You ever shot a man, Jack?" Paz said.

I just looked at him.

"He probably hasn't ever shot a gun," Wally Chen said.

I reached out and took the Colt from Peggy. Vanilla had a cigarette hanging from his lips.

"Flip the cigarette into the air," I said.

"What?"

"Flip your cigarette into the air," I said again.

"You're seriously going to hit that cigarette?" Little Joe said. Paz was smiling.

"Goddammit, flip it in the air while I still have something to shoot at!"

Vanilla stepped back. He took the cigarette between his thumb and forefinger.

"Ain't no way he can hit a cigarette," Peggy said.

"I do it every time," I said. It was dark but I could see Paz watching me. He seemed amused.

"I'll bet a hundred dollars he can," Paz said.

"No way," Peggy said.

"You on?"

"Sure."

Vanilla flipped the cigarette. It arched end over end, glowing in the night sky. I casually pointed the pistol at the moving glowing dot, and tracked it till it hit the asphalt in a shower of sparks.

I walked over to the cigarette and pointing the pistol down at it, I blew it to pieces.

I walked over to Peggy and twirled the pistol, turning it handle out and handed it to him.

Paz started laughing, "He never misses." He looked at Peggy, "You owe me a hundred bucks."

20

"That's cheating!" Elena said.

Blackhawk and Nacho were laughing.

"So, Paz thought it was funny?"

"Yeah, guess so. Thank God."

"What happened to the guy you were supposed to shoot?"

I shook my head, "They all just walked away, like they had forgotten all about him. By the time I got to Little Joe's car, he was gone."

We were at the El Patron. It was mid-morning and Elena had just come downstairs to the bar. She had performed the night before and she was religious about getting her nine hours. Anita's wedding reception was tonight and the place was resplendent with all things wedding. Anita was a friend of Elena's. Elena had desperately tried to get us involved, but it didn't take. Even though Anita appeared to have found a guy to make her happy, I don't think Elena had forgiven me yet.

Jimmy was in already. He must have sensed when Elena

would be down. He came from the back with a plate holding two poached eggs and a piece of dry toast. He sat it in front of Elena, then came down to the corner and refilled our coffee mugs. I could hear the back doors open with some clacking and banging. It was the cleaners. A moment later they moved by us, pushing their floor mates and vacuum cleaners. They usually started at the front and worked to the back. It would be a while before they would bother us. Everything about Blackhawk was kept immaculate. His body, his clothes, his cars, his woman and his nightclub. Even now he was wearing a crisp white shirt, pressed charcoal grey trousers, and a pair of gleaming black half boots, that probably cost more than a case of the twelve-year-old scotch he kept in the back.

"Tell me about the little homeless girl that wanted to give you a blowjob," Elena said, tearing a piece of toast and dabbing it into the egg. She innocently cocked her head to show she was completely engaged.

I looked at Blackhawk and he shrugged laughing again. "Elena and I have no secrets," he said. Nacho was amused.

"Some girl gave you a blowjob?" Nacho said.

"Nobody gave me a blowjob," I said. "She was on the street, and needed some money."

"So, you gave her money, but didn't get the blowjob?" Nacho said. "That was dumb."

"Nobody got a blowjob, and I didn't give her money. I took her down to Father Correa's."

"She gave Father Correa a blowjob?" Nacho said.

I just shook my head.

"Father Correa is a good man," Elena said. She looked at Blackhawk, "You should give him some money."

Blackhawk looked at me, "Yeah, I really should," he deadpanned.

"What time is Anita's reception tonight?" I said, to change the subject.

"You going to be here?" Elena asked, that old something flashing in her eyes.

"Am I invited?"

"You have to bring someone. It's couples only."

"What about me?" Nacho said.

Elena didn't glance at him, she was looking at me, "You are tending bar," she answered Nacho.

Nacho looked at Blackhawk, Blackhawk shrugged. What can you do?

"What if I don't have anyone," I said.

Elena swiveled to look at me full on. Uh oh, that wasn't smart.

"Of course, you don't have anyone." She swiveled back and used the rest of the toast to swab up the rest of the egg. "Anita is very sweet, and she liked you."

"I liked her too," I protested.

"Yes, you like her. So you get drunk and you tell her things that a man only tells a special woman. Some women wait a lifetime to hear these things. Then you disappear and leave her. And, those words are now only words."

"I don't remember that," I said. "I don't remember telling her those things."

"Of course, you don't remember. You were a drunken

fool. She is too good for you, and now she has found her man. And, you have lost her forever." Her eyes were flashing, "And, it serves you right."

Elena slid off her stool. She looked around the room, evaluating the decorations. She pointed at some bunting on the far wall. "That is too high," she looked back at me. "The reception starts at seven o'clock. Be sure to bring someone." She turned and walked across the dance floor to the stairs that led to the upstairs apartment.

After she disappeared through the upstairs door, I looked at Blackhawk.

"Is it really couples only?"

He grinned, "It is now."

21

"Are you friggin' kidding me?"

I had found Boyce watching the SanDunes from a half block down the street. She was sitting with a grocery cart, in the shade of some olive trees. The cart had all the stuff in it that a homeless person would have. I was sitting on the curb pretending to adjust my prosthetic.

"She said it was couples only," I said. "You're the only one I know that will go with me."

"I believe that," she grinned. "Who the hell is Anita?"

"Nobody."

"Nobody? But, you want to go to her reception?"

"Well, maybe not nobody. She's a friend of Elena's."

She looked at me, suspicious. "Why does Elena give a damn if you go to this girl's reception?"

"She's a friend of Elena's."

"I repeat, why does she give a damn?"

I was busy strapping my foot back on. "She was…," I started. "Elena….,.well, she tried to fix Anita up with me."

"That sounds like Elena. Trying to fix my emotional

problems with one hand, and fixing you up with the other. That still doesn't answer my question."

I stood up and dusted off my seat. "I think I'm being punished for not pursuing it. I got a little drunk and I don't know what I said, but whatever words I used, Anita took it seriously. Then when I didn't pursue it, I ended up in the doghouse."

Boyce was laughing. "God, Jackson, you are such a douche."

"Christ," I said. "I knew this was a bad idea." I started to walk away.

"What time does it start?"

I stopped. "I think at seven."

"I'll meet you there at seven-thirty. Never be the first one there."

"I can pick you up."

"Hell, no."

"It's no problem."

"I want my own wheels. Then I can leave when I want. Hell Jackson, you might get drunk and say those magic words." She started laughing.

I didn't laugh. "I'll meet you in the parking lot." I turned and walked away. It was a half block before I couldn't hear her laughter any more.

I still arrived at the El Patron early. I had made an excuse to Frank, telling him I wouldn't be in. I left the boarding house and walked to the car then drove to the boat. I opened it up for fresh air as I pulled out my one pair of Dockers, and a collared shirt. I was surely getting sick of the boarding house room. I knocked back three inches of bourbon for fortification and drove to El Patron. The whiskey didn't help. It had worn off before I even got there.

I was lucky to find a parking spot. I sat and watched for Boyce, and listened to NPR. Boyce was twenty minutes late. Which was on time for her. She had parked across the street and I spotted her coming into the lot. Her hair was down and bounced on her shoulders as she walked. She had a spaghetti-strap red dress on. The hem flounced just above her knees. She was wearing sexy high heels. The kind the young women called *fm pumps*. She looked really good. I know she did it on purpose. More fodder for Elena's cannon.

I got out and thumbed the remote to lock the Mustang. She saw me and was waiting by the front door. Duane was at the front door. He opened the door and held it.

"Ma'am," he nodded at Boyce. "How are you?"

"All healed up, Duane. Thanks for asking."

"Mr. Jackson," he said as I went by him.

"Jackson, Duane. Just Jackson."

The thumping of the bass was palpable as soon as we stepped inside. Blackhawk had closed the two other bars for the occasion. El Patron sported three bars, all with live music. One for the rock crowd, one was country, and the main large room was for Elena and her big salsa band. The salsa band was in full swing. Only missing Elena. We came down the hall to the main bar. The place was packed. The bride and groom were seated at a long table that held the wedding party. Elena was seated next to Anita. She was in a rose-colored gown that matched the other women in the wedding party. I immediately felt sorry for those other girls. Pretty, all of them, but not in Elena's league. Blackhawk and Nacho were behind the bar, helping Jimmy. They were busy. The bar was three deep. The dance floor was packed.

Boyce took my hand and dragged me out onto the dance floor. Back to the scene of the crime. I leaned into her ear, "You know I only have one foot."

She twirled and began dancing, "Men can't dance anyway," she said above the din, taking my hand and twirling under it. She was a good dancer.

I gave it my best try, but I felt like Fernando the bashful bull. It didn't really matter. The man was only on the dance floor so that the woman could dance. If the man wouldn't dance, that didn't matter either, the women would dance together, or alone if necessary. Finally, the band cut me a break and started a slow song. I started to turn toward the bar but Boyce caught my arm. She pulled me in close and wrapped an arm around my neck. We began to move together. She rested her head on my shoulder. Damn her.

I spoke into her ear. "You smell very nice. What brand of chicken skin did you use today?"

She pulled back to look me in the eye, "It's called j'adore. Do you like it?"

"It's unfair," I said.

She smiled and lay her head back on my shoulder. We finished out the song without me stepping on her foot. Who says men can't dance?

The place was packed. We wound our way through the masses and got close enough to the bar to catch Nacho's eye.

He held up a bottle of Dos Equis with a quizzical look. I held up two fingers. He popped the top from two of the green bottles. With one in each hand he leaned into the bar and spoke to the two young guys sitting there. The band had started up again so I couldn't hear what he said, but they didn't like it. He leaned a little closer, getting into their faces and said something else. The look on his face wasn't friendly. The two men reluctantly picked up their beers and slid off the bar stools. Nacho set a beer in front of each stool and waved us over. Boyce slid up on hers without a glance at the two guys. I glanced. It was met with a very unfriendly look.

Some things are universal. One is when people start clinking their glass with a piece of silverware the groom is supposed to kiss the bride. The clinking started and the groom leaned over and did his duty. He was a nice looking young man. Somewhat on the stocky side. Anita had been starving herself to fit into her dress. She looked very happy. I hoped she was.

Boyce leaned over, "How's it going with Paz?'

"They took me out on a run."

She hitched around, "Oh yeah?"

"Had a dealer skimming, decided to teach him a lesson."

"And took you along?"

I sipped my beer.

She set her bottle down and punched me in the shoulder. "That's great, Jackson."

"Yeah." I took another sip and set my bottle on the bar. Careful to keep it on the coaster.

She studied me, then leaned forward, "Are you going to

tell me what happened, or do I have to kick your ass?"

"Not much to happen. The guy was scared shitless as soon as they showed up. I guess Peggy is the crazy guy. Paz threatened to sic Peggy on him and the guy about wet himself."

Boyce nodded, "Yeah, Peggy is nuts." She kept looking at me, the noise of the crowd and band passing over us like a wave.

I took another drink and watched the crowd.

"Goddammit, are you going to tell me what happened?"

I swung around to look at the dance floor. Anita was out with her groom. They could really dance. "I shot a cigarette," I said.

Boyce leaned over, into my face, "You don't tell me what happened I am seriously going to punch you in the mouth!"

I was laughing. This pissed her off, she balled her fist and drew it back. "No, wait," I said, raising a hand to ward off the blow. "I did. I shot a cigarette."

She lowered her hand, and started laughing. "Jackson, I never know to believe you or not."

"Oh, believe it."

She picked up her beer and took a long drink, "okay, tell me."

We were interrupted by Jimmy setting a plastic champagne flute in front of everyone at the bar. Nacho was doing the same on the other side. Elena and Blackhawk were going through the crowd handing out the flutes to everyone else. The bridesmaids followed behind with bottles of tequila, pouring a little into each glass. Jimmy came back along the bar filling ours. He was pouring just about a shot into each flute but when he reached Boyce he winked and filled hers halfway up. I don't know that she noticed, she was watching the crowd.

I was grateful for the interruption. When everyone was served, Elena stepped up on the stage.

"Okay, everybody, settle down." She held her flute up. "A toast for Anita and Albert. May they have a long and wonderful marriage, and may they have many fat and happy babies. Saluda!"

Everyone shouted "Saluda" and tossed back the tequila.

One of the bridesmaids refilled Anita and Alberts glasses to the brim.

Boyce put her glass to her lips and took a sip. She looked at her glass. Boyce leaned into me and said, "I thought the tradition was for the best man to make the toast."

"This is Elena's show," I said.

"Of course," she said, still looking at her glass. She looked down the bar at Jimmy then looked at me, "You trying to get me drunk?"

I laughed, "I didn't pour that."

"Yeah, but your buddy did. So, tell me about shooting the cigarette."

So, I told her. While I was telling her, the band kicked it into high gear and everyone was dancing. While I talked, I watched one bridesmaid or another keep filling Anita's glass. I know impending trouble when I see it. It wasn't long before the wedding thing was gone and this had turned into one rowdy, full-on, bull-bitch of a party.

When I told Boyce about leaning over and shooting the cigarette she started laughing. "Paz didn't get pissed?"

I shrugged.

Anita and Alfred were tearing up the dance floor. Maybe it was me, but it seemed when their dancing brought them close to Boyce and me, Anita's laughter was just a little shriller. Boyce was still laughing about the cigarette when Anita's high heel caught on the hem of her layered dress and she stumbled, then fell hard. She landed just a few feet from us. She struggled to her feet with Albert trying to help her. She saw Boyce laughing. She launched herself at Boyce.

"You bitch! You think this is funny?"

Boyce slid sideways off her stool and shoved Anita. Anita's momentum crashed her into me. I had to grapple with her to keep her from hitting the floor again. She started screaming and hitting me with both hands.

I think she was calling me names but it was one unintelligible howl. I was trying to keep her from going to the floor, and defend myself at the same time. One of her blows caught me on the ear and it stung like hell.

By now we were surrounded. Albert came up behind Anita and I tried to leverage her into his arms. She was screaming that I had molested her. It was in Spanish, but that's sure what it sounded like. Albert pulled her off me and handed her off to a burly guy with a family resemblance to the bride. Albert took a big round house swing at me and I slid sideways and bopped him in the nose. A gush of blood went down his lacey white wedding shirt.

I got blindsided by a groomsman and I staggered into the

bar. Nacho vaulted the bar like a collegiate gymnast over a vaulting horse. Landing, he smashed himself into what, by now, had turned into a giant melee. He grabbed the guy that had blindsided me and slung him into a mass of swinging arms and kicking legs. I took shelter, squatting between the two stools Boyce and I had occupied. She was nowhere in sight. With my back to the bar, I had a remarkable view. Now everyone was into it. There weren't any sides, people, men and women, were punching and kicking whoever was close. Finally, I saw Blackhawk working his way along the back wall. He stepped up on the bandstand, where the musicians had been busy defending themselves by keeping people off of it. He spoke to the lead guy. The guy with the big guitar. That guy shouted orders to the other musicians and they broke into a loud rendition of *Himno Nacional Mexicano*. The Mexican national anthem.

Slowly but surely, the fighting began to diminish until all were standing, facing the bandstand. Then one of the groomsmen began to cheer, and they all began to cheer.

I climbed to my feet and looked around for Boyce.

She and Elena were halfway up the stairs to the second landing. Sitting on the steps, they each had a glass of tequila. Their heads were together, and they were laughing.

Boyce saw me looking and raised her glass in a toast. Elena's look wasn't as friendly.

22

Blackhawk handed me the bottle of water I had asked for. We were above the bar in the apartment he and Elena shared. It was two in the morning. The party was over. Nacho was stretched out on the floor asleep. Elena and Boyce were in the back. They were still dressed in their wedding reception finery. Elena was having Boyce try on some shoes Elena was getting rid of. She had owned them so long she was tired of them. They were at least two months old.

Blackhawk fixed a single malt scotch on ice and brought it over. His first drink of the night. He stretched out on the oversized sofa and swirled the scotch over the ice. I was in the fat leather chair with the fat leather ottoman. I drank half the bottle of water.

"God, I'm glad that is over with," Blackhawk said.

"How did you get wrangled into doing it in the first place?"

He turned his head to me and cocked an eyebrow.

I smiled, "Oh yeah."

"How much longer you going to be messing with Paz?"

"Till we have him with his hand in the cookie jar."

"Hard to do," Blackhawk said. "He doesn't get his hands dirty. That's what those other guys are for."

"I'll think of something. I just have to earn a little more trust."

"Hard to do while keeping your hands clean."

"Yeah," I agreed.

"So, you ready to get your hands dirty."

"I think the reason Mendoza asked me to do this is because I'm willing to get my hands dirty."

"True that."

"I just have to find the right mud to wallow in."

Boyce and Elena came back into the room. Boyce was carrying a pair of very sparkly high heels. She came over and sat on the arm of my chair. She kicked off her pumps and put on the new ones. She walked around the room, doing a couple of twirls.

"How do they look?" she said to no one in particular.

"They are sexy," Elena said. She looked at me, "Don't you think they are sexy, Jackson?"

"Oh, yeah. Very sexy," I said.

Nacho lifted his head, "Sexy as hell," he said. He rolled to his side and closed his eyes.

"Why don't you get up and go home," Elena said.

"I'm too tired," Nacho said.

"Go home, Nacho," Blackhawk said.

Nacho lumbered to his feet and stretched.

I got to my feet, "Time for me to go," I said.

"Me too," Boyce said.

Boyce hugged Elena and Blackhawk and I hugged Elena. She hugged me back and I felt I had escaped something. We followed Nacho down the stairs.

The outside air was warm. The parking lot was empty except for my Mustang sitting out by the street. Blackhawk's Jag and Nacho's Jeep were nosed up against the building.

Boyce hugged Nacho. He climbed into his Jeep, started it up, and drove away. I walked Boyce through the asphalt lot, then across the street to where her little Miata was parked. She beeped the door lock open.

She turned to look at me. There was a small twinkle in her eye.

"Helluva party," she said.

"Hell of a party."

"You going back to the boarding house?"

"Hell no. I'm going to the boat. I need a break."

She stood there looking at me. The street lights softened her face and glinted off her dark hair.

"I could use a break myself," she said.

She hugged me around the neck and held on a little longer than was necessary. She kissed me on the cheek. I held the door as she climbed in. She started the Miata and drove away.

The drive back to the boat seemed to take forever. I had the windows down, letting the wind blow through the car. The moon was up and late-night traffic was light. After what seemed like forever I pulled into the long entrance to the marina, past the parking lot for the tourists and down to my parking spot. My headlights picked up the Miata in my parking spot. I pulled up beside it and Boyce was leaning against her car. I turned the Mustang off and stepped out.

"Break time," Boyce said.

23

By the time I came into the SanDunes there were just a few customers left. Only Little Joe and Wally Chen were sitting at the back. I had seen Peggy driving Paz away when I was still a half block away. As I slid up on my barstool, Wally Chen stood, then walked out past me without a glance. Little Joe came down and sat beside me. He signaled to Frank. Frank brought him a rock glass of whiskey. He set a beer in front of me.

Little Joe took a drink, then swiveled to look at me. He was a big guy. He would be a tussle.

"Paz thought you were pretty funny, shooting that cigarette."

There was nothing to say to that, so I just smiled.

"Yeah, that was pretty funny," he said. He took another sip of his drink. "Don't get too cute with Paz. You get cute he'll shoot you in the gut then have us clean it up."

"Copy that," I said. "But, I figured it was better to shoot the cigarette than that guy."

He looked at me, "You have a problem shooting that guy?"

"Way above my pay grade." I said. "You guys pay me to clean this bar, not to shoot your thieves."

"You'd shoot him if we paid you right?"

"There is a whole lot of *If* in there."

"You ever shoot anyone?"

"Probably, I think so. I shot at some guys, I must have hit one or two."

He smiled, "In the Army?"

I nodded, "Marines."

"Iraq?"

"Afghanistan."

"Who were you with?"

This was the tricky part. Was he over there? Would he know one unit from another?

"Started with 1st Battalion," I said taking a drink. "3rd Marines. Ended up with 66 Military Police Unit." I looked at him, "Were you over there?"

"Naw. Shit, I don't do soldier stuff. So, you were a cop?"

"Military cop."

"How'd you end up in the Marines?"

I turned to look at the room, my back to the bar. "Barely made it through high school. When I got out I had a choice of working in a factory or joining up. Figured I wanted to see the world more than work in some old factory."

"Did you see the world?"

"At first, yeah, guess so. Then the world turned out to be nothing but wide-open deserts with nothing but dirt, heat, rocks and little sand nits that would eat the hell out of you. Brown people that looked at you like you were lice."

"That where you lost your foot?"

"Yeah. It's still over there somewhere. Probably have a toenail left in Helmand Province. I was told they looked for it but never found it. Probably in tiny pieces."

"Tough luck."

"Tough luck was them that came back in a body bag." I finished my beer. I lay it on its side so Frank wouldn't bring me another one. I turned back around and looked at him. "You ever in the service."

He laughed, "Hell no. I've been in my current profession since I was fourteen."

"Current profession? Professional thug?"

He laughed again. "Pays better than that factory."

He was looking at me now. Serious. "I think Paz likes you."

This took me aback.

"I don't know whether to be flattered or frightened."

"You handled yourself pretty good."

"I ain't that tough. But I did grow up in a tough neighborhood. You didn't get tough enough, you got eaten alive."

"Where was that?"

"Place in Illinois. Down state from Chicago. Town called Decatur. Factory town. Ended up in an orphanage there. Was on the streets early."

"What happened to your parents?"

"Car wreck."

"No brothers or sisters?"

"Nope."

"Nobody?"

"Nope."

"Tough."

I shrugged. Old story. "How about you?"

His turn to shrug. "I'm a Phoenix native. Born at St. Joe's. Grew up down around lower Buckeye. Tough neighborhood."

"High school?"

"Dropped out when I realized I could make more money on the streets than the stiffs working 9 to 5."

"How'd you meet Paz?"

He turned to signal Frank for another drink. "Just met him out there. I was dealing, he was my supplier. Took a liking to each other."

"Buddies?"

He shrugged again. Frank set the drink in front of him. He took a light drink. "Working buddies," he said. He looked at me, "Make no mistake. I work for Paz like everyone else. I cross him, he'll shoot me as fast as anyone else. Or, feed me to Peggy."

"You worried about Peggy?"

"Peggy's a loon. He won't just shoot you. He'll shoot you in the legs, then kick you to death."

I looked down at Frank. "How about old Frank there," I said. "Was he dealing for Paz?"

He shook his head, "Naw. Frank owned this place. Paz made him an offer, and kept him on." Again, he looked at me, "Frank went along with us the other night but that's unusual. He normally sticks to the bar."

"How about Wally? What's his story?"

I could feel the change in him. He looked at me. "You ask too many questions."

I shrugged, "Sorry. Just killing time till it's time to clean."

He tossed his drink back and slid off the stool. "Be sure to get the women's toilet good. Women won't come in here with a bad toilet."

I saluted, "Will do boss."

He waved at Frank and walked out.

24

It was getting muggy. Hot and muggy, a terrible combination. The TV in the bar had been predicting thunderstorms all week. With the wind picking up, I had hurriedly walked the five blocks to the closest grocery store, and bought a few items that I kept in my room. Mrs. Haggerty let me keep a couple of items in her refrigerator, but I was forbidden to mention this to the other tenants. After all, where would it end? When I got back to the boarding house there was a strange car backing out of the dirt driveway. There was a young man in a suit at the wheel. One of those slick guys, dark hair slicked straight back. Expensive suit. He had lit a cigarette. He didn't seem to notice that I was even there. I had to stop walking to let him back down into the street. Without a look, he had driven away. It was a medium sized Buick. Very sterile, very functional. I had automatically clicked on his license plate.

I came down the front stairs with the creamer for the refrigerator. I also carried my oversized mug of coffee to pour it in. It was a large mug because I only made one mug at a time and the smaller cups didn't get it. I really didn't like powdered creamer, so I made the trek to the kitchen every day.

Mrs. Haggerty and Mrs. Eberly were at the dining table, their heads close together. They seemed unusually excited. I moved into the kitchen and poured the creamer into my coffee, then put it away in the frig. I could barely hear them but I did catch Mrs. Eberly say, in a conspiratorial tone, "I can't believe he had that much money."

I carried my mug back in, "Who had money? That kid that just left?" I said.

They looked up, flustered.

"I didn't know you heard me," Mrs. Eberly said, with a mild flush.

"I'm sorry," I said. "I don't mean to eavesdrop. None of my business."

Mrs. Haggerty patted Mrs. Eberle on the hand. "Tell Jack about it. He's a good boy. He won't say anything."

"Don't tell me anything unless you want to," I said.

"Well, I would appreciate it if you don't say anything, but that young man that just left is from the bank. It seems Mr. Eberle left an account behind that I knew nothing about."

"And, it has a lot of money in it," Mrs. Haggerty said, her eyes bright.

I pulled a chair out, and sat on it.

"How can it be you didn't know about it?" I said, sipping the coffee.

"Mr. Burns, that young man, said it was an abandoned

account. He says they were about to close it out because of how long it's been without activity, and they couldn't find anyone it might be attached to."

"This is your bank?"

"Oh yes."

"They didn't know this was your husband?"

"Mr. Burns said he overheard the teller use my name the last time I was in, oh, when was that Mildred?"

"A week ago, Tuesday, we went to the mall that day," Mrs. Haggerty said.

"Yes, over a week ago. He was working on some of the abandoned accounts and recognized the last name and heard my last name and remembered that one of the accounts had the same name."

"Why couldn't they identify you as the wife."

She smiled sheepishly. She shook her head.

"My husband hated his name. He was born Elwood Merle Eberly. He hated it. So early on, I think he said in the second grade, he took the EL and MER and called himself Elmer. When he was eighteen he changed it legally. We had been married over forty years before he told me about his name. It was when his hometown courthouse burned down. He told me his birth certificate burned with it. You see," she said, leaning toward me, "He had no family."

"None?"

"No one. His parents died when he was in the service. His mother died and then two months later his father followed. He said his dad just didn't want to go on. He had no brothers or sisters. Didn't even have Uncles or Aunts or cousins, or anything. He had the account under Elwood Merle Eberly."

"Why did he have this account?"

Now she actually flushed. The color running down her neck and into the patterned housedress she wore. She hesitated.

Mrs. Haggerty patted her hand again. "It's okay honey. There's nothing wrong with this. He was a good man."

Again, Mrs. Eberly leaned toward me. She glanced around and lowered her voice. "Mr. Eberly liked to gamble. During the season, he was out betting on the ponies at Turf Paradise, just about every weekend. He always told me he broke even. He didn't drink or smoke, so I always let him have this one little vice. We always got by okay, so I let him do this one thing."

"He did better than break even," Mrs. Haggerty said. "That young man said there was thirty thousand dollars in that account."

"Holy cow!" I said. I always liked that exclamation. It worked in just about every situation. "So, this Mr. Burns figured out that Elwood Merle was your Elmer?"

"He said he suspected it. That's when he came to see me. So, when I told him about Elmer's real name he got so excited."

"But, there was a problem," I said

"Yes, there was," said Mrs. Haggerty. "They have no way to prove that Eunice was married to Elwood Merle Eberly."

"No way?"

"None," said Mrs. Eberly. "Everything I have, everything we have in storage, just everything says my husband's name was Elmer."

"So, you can't get the money?"

She smiled slyly. "Mr. Burns has figured out a way."

Now I leaned forward. "That's great," I said. "How is he going to do that."

"Well," Mrs. Eberly said, drawing herself up, "I had a CD at the bank that had thirty thousand in it. So, Mr. Burns said that if I combined my money with Elmer's, then the account automatically becomes a joint account."

"You *had* a CD??"

"Well, yesterday I drew the money out, and Mr. Burns just now picked it up to take to the bank."

I looked out the window, thinking. "Why did you draw it out? Why didn't you just transfer it at the bank?"

"That's what I asked," Mrs. Haggerty said.

Mrs. Eberly said, "Mr. Burns said that even though everything is completely on the up and up, if we did anything other than a cash transaction, it would cause questions, and someone would stick their nose in, raise questions about my husband's name. Like I said, I can't prove I'm really married to Elwood Merle. And since there's no way to prove that, it was just easier this way. It's not like I'm taking someone else's money," she said firmly.

"You sure you can trust this Mr. Burns?"

"Oh, yes. I called the bank and they verified he was an officer of the bank."

I had spied the business card lying on the table. I picked it up.

"Is this the bank number you called."

"Yes. You see the address there," she pointed at the

bottom of the card. "That's my branch."

I set the card back on the table, then stood. I took the cup into the kitchen, poured out the remaining coffee, and rinsed the cup.

"Now, Jack," Mrs. Haggerty said through the door. "This is nobody's business but Eunice's."

"Yes, ma'am," I said, moving through the dining room and started up the stairs. "Mum's the word."

I had memorized the bank number from the business card. When I got to my room, I called it. The number rang and rang, then notified me the party had not set up their voice mail box. I disconnected. I knew that by tomorrow the number would be out of service.

I called Mendoza. He answered on the first ring.

"I need you to run a license number for me," I said without preliminaries.

"Why?" he said.

"There's a guy grifting an old lady at my boarding house." I explained it to him.

"I'll give it to Vice."

"No, I'll take care of it. This is personal."

"Everything with you is personal."

"You ever felt that way?"

"Everyday. What's the number?"

I gave it to him. He hung up.

I put the phone in my pocket and lay back on the bed. I was dozing when the phone vibrated, jolting me awake. It was Mendoza.

"It's a rental," he said.

"Can we find out who rented it?"

"I called them."

"And?"

"The clerk told me it was privileged information, and she couldn't divulge it over the phone."

"Did you explain you are a Captain?"

"Yeah, for some reason that didn't persuade her. It didn't persuade her boss either."

"How do we get the guy's name?"

"I sent a car out to talk with them."

"That'll do it?"

"Yep."

"How do you know?"

"The guy I sent has been a street cop for twenty-years. He'll get the info."

"You sure?"

"I'm a Captain. I'm always sure."

25

The weather was rapidly turning. Flash flood warnings were out for all of Maricopa County. I decided to run out to the boat to make sure it was secure. By the time I got the Mustang on the road the wind was whipping sideways with rain drops the size of quarters.

When I pulled into my reserved parking spot, the rain was pouring. Thank God Danny was running the shuttle. All dressed in yellow foul weather gear, including the plastic cover for his cowboy hat. He dropped me at the gate to my dock. I gave him a five for his troubles. By the time I stepped on board, and disconnected the alarm, I was soaked.

I had turned the air off while I was at the boarding house, and the inside was steamy. I turned the air all the way to high, turned on the galley lights, then stepped back out into the storm. I checked the mooring, loosening the mooring lines so that the bouncing swells didn't strain the brackets. I checked the bumpers. I climbed to topside and made sure all the lounge chairs and cushions were fastened down, or stored in the large lockers.

Satisfied, I went back into the lounge and dripped on the carpet. I pulled the blackout curtains back so I could watch the storm. Storms like this are so unusual here, they are fascinating. I stepped out of my sodden clothes, wadded them into a ball, and threw them into the stacked washer. I threw in a pod of laundry soap and fired it up. I toweled off, put on dry clothes, and fixed a drink.

I was in the master stateroom, watching the waves of rain punish the lake when my phone rang. It was Mendoza.

"I'm sending you a text with an attachment. We got a copy of his driver's license with his address.

"Thanks," I said, but he had already disconnected.

I felt the boat shift. I stood very still. It shifted again. I reached behind the bedside table and lifted the Ruger from the magnet that held it. I moved into the galley, holding the gun next to my leg.

Out on the bow was a wet Pete Dunn unsuccessfully hiding under an umbrella. I lay the Ruger behind the toaster, and opened the front sliding door. He came in, turning to shake the umbrella and collapsing it.

"Saw your lights, hope it's okay if I come over."

"It's not a fit night out for man nor beast."

"Hey, W.C. Fields. I'd have thought you would be too young for that."

"Old movies and TV shows were the only things we were allowed to watch when I was a kid at the home. Come on in."

"I feel like a wet dog."

We went into the galley where the floor was linoleum. I

took the umbrella and lay it on the counter. "I've already fixed a drink; would you like one?"

"Love it. I was starting to go stir crazy, so when I saw your light, I took a chance you wouldn't mind company."

"Happy to have you, what would you like?"

"Whatever you're having."

I fixed the drink and as I was handing it to him my phone buzzed. I looked at it and saw it was the text from Mendoza. I clicked it open. It had a driver's license attached. Clyde Slick who said his name was Burns was really Grover Hilland. The address on the license was in Scottsdale. I held it out to show Pete.

"This is a real, honest to God, grifter."

He took the phone and studied it.

"Who's he grifting?"

I told him the story.

"Sounds like a variation of the old fashion pigeon drop. These women are really naive."

"That and greedy. That's what guys like him count on. I'm surprised you know what a pigeon drop is."

"You learn a lot in Hollywood."

The pigeon drop was an old scam that utilized what every scam utilizes, greed. The grifter arranges it so he and the mark come upon a wallet stuffed with money at the same time. There is no identification. They agree to each put up a large sum of good faith money while they wait for it to be claimed. They include their money with the found money, and wait three days for the true owner to announce themselves. If the owner doesn't show, they'll split the money. The grifter wraps it all up with lots of tape, makes a big deal of signing across the tape, and gives it to the mark to hold. They agree to meet back at the same place in three days. Of course, whenever the mark opens the package, he will find nothing but newspaper, and the grifter is long gone.

"You think this guy still has their money?"

"Yeah I do. Where, is the question."

"Are you going to take it back?"

"Forcibly taking it back would be hard to do. He's probably got it in a bank by now. I'm going to go one better. I'm going to get their money back, and a chunk of his."

"How?"

"I'll figure it out. Nobody is greedier than a grifter."

"Can I help."

I took a drink and looked at him.

"I'm really bored," he said.

I thought about it.

Finally I said, "I'm going to need to know everything I can find out about this guy. I'm working on that other thing right now, so it would be difficult for me to get away and do the digging. I'll need someone computer savvy who could get into this guy's social media. Find out what kind of dirt bag he really is. Then follow this guy around for a week. Figure out his habits."

"Pete Dunn, private eye," he said with a grin.

"If you get caught, it might get hairy."

"I won't get caught."

Again, I looked at him for a long moment. Then I smiled, "Do you have a fedora and a trench coat?"

26

Over the next few days, Paz sent me out with the guys three times. I didn't do anything but stand around while they did their thing. Usually, collecting money. It didn't seem to change my pay grade. I still cleaned the toilets at night. I still met Boyce by the garbage bins and told her what I knew, which was not much. She still smelled bad.

This night I was sitting at my barstool waiting for Frank to close the place. There were only a couple of customers. At the other end of the bar, Wally Chen and Peggy were playing cards with Little Joe watching. Vanilla came in and went straight to the back. The other three just glanced at him. A moment later he and Paz came from the back. Paz glanced my way, then they sat at the table with the other three. Paz spoke softly, and I couldn't hear what was said. The four men leaned in, hanging on every word. A thrill of alarm went through me when Wally Chen looked up, directly at me. After a brief discussion, Little Joe and Chen stood and came down the bar to me.

"I've got an errand to run," Little Joe said. "Paz wants you to come with me."

"I'm supposed to clean," I said.

"It'll keep till tomorrow," he said. I felt relieved. This sounded like I would have a tomorrow. I swallowed the last of the beer I'd been nursing and followed them out. We took Little Joe's car. Little Joe climbed in the driver's seat, with Chen in the back. I took the front passenger seat. I didn't like having Chen behind me, but not much to do about it.

We drove east until we hit I 17 then we went south for a while.

I knew it would be natural for me to ask, so I asked, "Where we going?"

Neither of them said anything, so I lapsed into silence. Little Joe finally pulled off the Freeway and traveled south. I could have thrown a rock and hit the El Patron, but we continued on south. Then suddenly I knew where we were going. Into Bono Pike's territory.

Of course, I was not supposed to know this, so I just serenely gazed out the window. When we reached the industrial park where Pike had his headquarters, Little Joe slowed, and as we drove past, both Little Joe and Chen studied the place intently. The place was dark and the streets were deserted. Everyone that worked in the industrial park were long gone home. There were no lights at Pike's except for street lights. As we passed I could see security lights at the back of the deserted parking lot. Little Joe went two more blocks then did a U-turn and pulled into a deserted parking lot. He drove to the back and came to a halt beside some large dumpsters. He angled the car under a security light. He and Chen climbed out, so I followed.

Little Joe went to the back of the car and popped the trunk open. He reached in and brought out an AR-15 and handed it to Chen. Then he brought out another and handed it to me.

"You know what this is?" Little Joe said.

"Sure, AR-15," I said.

"You were in the Army, just like a M-16," Chen said.

"Marines," I said. "But no, it's not. The hammer and trigger are designed differently. And, some of it is milled differently so the parts aren't interchangeable."

Little Joe smiled, Chen didn't. Little Joe looked at Chen, "He knows his guns." He shut the trunk lid and went back to the driver's side. "Climb in back with Wally," he said, then slid into the driver's seat.

I went around and climbed in back.

Little Joe drove us back to Pike's place. He pulled into the empty parking lot and slowly cruised around to the back. The security lights mounted above the large rolling door illuminated the back area. The door was the size of a double car garage. Little Joe kept the car back away from the building as far as he could get. He backed and filled until we were pointed back the way we had come. He stopped, and he and Chen climbed out. I followed, not sure what we were doing.

Without looking at me, Little Joe said, "Paz wanted to send a message." Now he looked across the top of the car at me. "Remember those assholes that tried to blow us up? This is where they hang out." He nodded to Chen.

Chen opened fire, raking bullets across the back of the

building, ricocheting off the metal door, sending sparks across the back. Chen kept firing until his clip was empty. I just stood there.

With the explosions still ringing in my ears, Little Joe pointed at me, "Go ahead. Shoot."

"I told you, it's above my pay grade."

"Consider yourself promoted. Go ahead, light it up."

I racked the round in and began raking fire across the building. The rifle pulled up and to the right. I compensated and took out the two lights that Chen had left. I stopped before I had used up all my rounds. I knew they couldn't tell. Nobody counts automatic fire rounds.

Little Joe was grinning. Suddenly, the back door flew open and a dark figure came out, firing a pistol as he came. The rounds slammed into Little Joe's car, hitting one of the headlights. Little Joe yelped and ducked down. Chen was reaching for his hip pistol. The man took a shooters stance and was aiming at Little Joe. I had no choice, I shot him. He went down. I had tried to hit him in the legs, but I couldn't tell.

All three of us scrambled back into the car, and Little Joe left an inch of rubber all the way through the parking lot. He missed the driveway and banged over the curb. I was looking out the back. Two more dark figures came running out, shooting at us. But, in a second, we were gone.

No one said anything as we sped through the night.

Finally, Little Joe said, "Goddammit, no one was supposed to be there."

"Vanilla said they had all left," Chen said. "Their cars must have been inside."

"I'm going to kick his ass myself," Little Joe said. Then he began to laugh, "Hey, that was kinda fun." He looked over his shoulder, back at me, "You did good, kid."

"Saved your ass," Chen said, looking out his window.

Little Joe didn't reply to that. He drove the back roads back to the bar. No sense getting stopped for missing a headlight with bullet holes in the car. No one spoke all the way back.

Paz, Vanilla and Peggy were at the bar, waiting. Frank was gone. Little Joe stormed in the bar and went straight to Vanilla. He grabbed him by the lapels and slung him against the pool table.

"You son of a bitch, you said no one would be there."

Vanilla held his hands up and out, as if to ward the big man off. "There wasn't anyone there, I swear it."

"The hell you say. They shot the shit out of my car. Almost got me."

"Would have, if it hadn't been for Jack," Wally Chen said quietly.

"What happened?" Paz said.

Little Joe was calming down. "We did what you said. Wally and Jack used the AK's to shoot the place up, but next thing you know those assholes came out shooting. They jacked my car good."

"They get a look at you?" Paz asked.

Little Joe looked at the floor. Wally Chen averted his eyes.

Paz turned to me, "They get a look at you?"

I nodded, "Yeah, they got a look at us."

Paz looked at Little Joe, "Well, shit. You can't do something simple?"

As the words came out of his mouth, we all heard the screeching of multiple cars piling into the SanDunes parking lot. We all turned and looked toward the door. I heard a car door slam and I yelled, "Get down!"

I vaulted the bar as the others scrambled for cover. Immediately, the bar exploded into a non-stop barrage of gunfire. Bullets raked through the door and walls and chewed up everything in sight. Bottles exploded, and the mirror came crashing down. Barstools were knocked on their sides. I made myself as small as possible. Then as suddenly as it had started, it finished. A moment later I could hear cars roaring off into the night.

I was covered with shards of glass. Still down low, and out of sight, I picked up one of the larger pieces and nicked my forehead about an inch above my eyebrows. The blood immediately began to flow. It was an old Carny trick. When the Carny strongman wanted it to look as if the local tough guy was really giving him a beating, he would nick himself with a hidden razor blade, and it would appear the local guy was beating him bloody. That's when the other Carny's would up the betting odds.

I stood, brushing the broken glass off of me. Slowly, the others stood, they all held a pistol except me. No one seemed hurt, but the bar was a mess.

"Make sure they're gone," Paz said to no one in particular. Peggy lumbered to the broken door and cautiously stepped outside. A moment later he was back.

"They're gone," he said.

Paz looked at me. "Jesus Christ, you been shot?"

I wiped my hand across my face. It came away bloody. "I'm okay," I said.

"Well, you look like hell." Paz looked at Little Joe, "Get someone in here tomorrow. Get this place fixed up."

27

It turned out it took three days to repair the damage to SanDunes, so Paz closed the bar for the duration. I took the opportunity to go back to the boat. The sun was setting and Blackhawk, Pete Dunn and I were sitting up top drinking Dos Equis.

"So, they followed you back to SanDunes?" Pete said.

"Didn't have to follow," Blackhawk said. "They already knew who and where they were." He took a drink and stretched his legs out in front of him. "Smart to counterpunch so fast. None of you were ready for that."

"No, we weren't," I said. "But, the good thing is that it was so fast, we didn't have a chance to fight back."

"Meaning, no one got hurt?" Pete said.

"Meaning just that." I looked at Pete. "So, have you found anything out about our thief?"

"Guy's a hot dog. A real ladies man. Drives a Dodge Challenger like a maniac. He trolls older women on Facebook. Takes them out, gets them drunk, goes back to their place. I'm guessing he knocks them out with some kind of date drug, then robs them. One night I staked him out…"

"Staked him out," Blackhawk smiled.

"Yeah, sounds cool doesn't it," Pete grinned. "Anyway, I sat across the street after he had taken the woman back to her place. About a half an hour later the lights started going on all over the house, and a half hour after that he left. Leaving the lights on."

I was watching some late water skiers, out across the water. The boat didn't have the proper lights for night running. I glanced over to the buoy that I normally swam to. I hadn't been swimming much and I was feeling sluggish. "Just the older gals? No sweet young things?"

"He saves that for the weekend."

I looked at him, he had my attention.

Pete seemed pleased with himself. "Every weekend he goes clubbing, and he always scores. He's pretty sly."

"Sly?" Blackhawk said.

"He likes the young hook-up joints in Scottsdale on the weekends."

"Hook up joints?" I said. I looked at Blackhawk, "You know any hook up joints?"

"Elena won't let me," he said.

"Places like The Vig, or the Devil's Martini. Dance clubs like Axis/Radius," Pete continued.

"You ever heard of those?" I asked Blackhawk.

"Elena won't let me," he said.

"So, what's the sly part?" I asked.

"Both times I went in behind him," he glanced at me, "don't worry, I waited a good twenty minutes and each time

I looked different. He goes in later, after everyone else has had plenty to drink. Each time he walks out with a girl. The sly part is that he would target a group of girls, usually co-eds out on the night."

"What's sly about that."

"Nothing, except he always targeted the one girl that no one else was hitting on. These are dance clubs. And, the girls are there to dance. But, there is always one girl in a group that doesn't get the attention, and that's the one he would hit on. Worked every time."

"Wasn't particular," Blackhawk said.

"But very successful. And, believe me, he's a damn good dancer. He wouldn't have any trouble getting any of the girls to dance. The older gals are for the money. The younger ones for recreation."

"Even the homely ones."

"They aren't homely," Pete said. "If I had to assign a characteristic, they are just young and awkward. They all lack a certain sophistication or sexual maturity the others have."

"How do you know that?"

"You can tell. Sometimes how they dress. You know the girls that are out trolling, they dress like it. Also, I told you, I've spent a lot of time in Hollywood. There, the girls in the clubs are predators and they act like it. The girls this guy picks could have been just off the farm. New to college, haven't been around much yet."

"Does he always go to these same places?"

"Every weekend. The bartenders know his name."

"Grover?"

"No. Tommy. Goes by Tommy. His credit card is Grover T. Hilland. I got a look at a slip while he was dancing. That's how I found his Facebook page. No one named Grover Hilland is on the internet. But, Tommy Hilland has lots of friends."

"Yeah," I said, watching the boat disappear into the distance. "Tommy is a safe name. Nobody bad was ever named Tommy."

"Tommy gun." Blackhawk said.

"That's a knee slapper." I looked at Pete, "Does he hang with any guys?"

"Never saw it. He lives in a condo in downtown Phoenix. A high rise. Pays for parking in a parking garage. Except when he's working or clubbing, that's where he always is."

Blackhawk stood. As he came out of his chair he looked lithe and smooth, like a cat moving. A big cat. He collected our empties and went to the ice locker located by the cockpit. He got three more beers, popped the caps and brought them back to us. The sun was almost down, some of the eastern stars were out.

"How are you going to take him?" Blackhawk asked, settling into his chair again.

"I haven't figured it out yet, but I'm going to make him beg for it."

"Greed," said Blackhawk. "The guy likes having money, he just doesn't want to work for it. They all want something for nothing. That's why they do what they do."

"There is an old adage, that the easiest guy to sell is a

salesman, and the easiest guy to grift is a grifter," I said.

"How are you going to get close to this guy. Close enough to draw him in, I mean," Pete asked. "Like I said, he has no guy friends. While he's at these bars he doesn't talk to anyone, not about football, nothing. Just to the girls, and usually to the one he's selected."

"Yeah," Blackhawk smiled at me. "How you gonna do that?"

I took a long drink, thinking about it.

"I'll make him come to me."

28

The first day the SanDunes reopened, Paz called Frank and me back to his office. Little Joe, Peggy and Wally Chen were there. It made the small room crowded. The guys had all the chairs, so I found a spot on the wall and leaned against it.

Paz glanced at me, then spoke to Frank, "I'm going to be using Jack, so you need to find another janitor."

Oh, glorious promotion.

Frank grimaced then shrugged, "Anything else?"

"No," Paz said. Frank turned and left.

Paz leaned back in his chair and looked at me. "I'm starting you at a thousand a week. You hang with Little Joe for a couple of weeks, then we'll see."

"Sounds good to me," I said. "Thanks."

Paz shrugged, like it was nothing, and to him it probably wasn't. He turned to the other guys, "What're we going to do about Pike?"

"Hit the son of a bitch," Peggy said. "Take him out."

"He's ready for us now," Wally Chen said. "They're probably already moved out of that place."

"Wally's right," Little Joe said. "It's going to be tougher now."

Paz looked at me, "What do you think?"

I shrugged, "What did you expect, shooting up their little clubhouse? You thought they'd just surrender?"

Little Joe shifted uncomfortably. Wally Chen looked at the floor. Paz held his gaze on me. After an uncomfortable silence Paz said, "So, what would you do?"

"Hold your friends close, hold your enemy's closer," I said.

"What the fuck does that mean?" Peggy said.

"Shut up," Paz said. He hadn't taken his eyes off of me. "Elaborate," he said.

Elaborate? Wow.

"Germany and Japan."

Now Wally Chen was looking at me like I was crazy.

I kept talking. "At one time, we were trying to destroy both of those guys. We beat the shit out of them, but now they are two of our closest allies in the world."

Paz leaned back in his chair, watching me.

"I say we make Pike an ally."

Paz looked puzzled. "How do we do that?"

"Make him an offer he can't refuse. After we make it clear he can't hide, and we make it clear we could cause him a world of hurt, offer to make him your partner. Throw a ton of money at him. Give him autonomy. Then, when his guard is down, take him out. Or, leave him alone if you want."

"What's that ah-tawn-no shit?" Peggy said.

"Autonomy, let him run his own shop," Wally Chen said.

"This world of hurt," Paz said. "How do you go about doing that?"

"You show him you are too big to whip. What's he got? He has dealers in his area, moving grass and heroin and opioids? Like you?"

"He ain't nearly as big as me," Paz said.

"Of course. But he wants to be. But I'll bet he knows he can't win a full-scale war. So, we prove that to him. Hit his supply chain. Scare off some of his dealers. Take out a couple of his main guys. Then make him an offer he can't refuse."

Paz looked at Little Joe, "I thought you said this guy was just some bar bum."

Wally Chen was studying me intently.

Little Joe shrugged his massive shoulders. "You never know."

"I was in the service," I said. "I did three tours in Afghanistan. I ended up a Sergeant in the M.P.'s. The Army is lousy keeping track of their supplies, so it was easy to siphon stuff off for a profit. I had a half million in a footlocker, then I lost the foot. They packed me up and shipped me to Germany, and I never saw the footlocker again. But, I saw a lot of tribal shit while I was over there. This is basically the same thing. The tribes that survived were the ones that banded together."

Paz was thinking. "I like it," he said. "I get us joined up, then I take the asshole out and I'm left with both pieces." He looked at Little Joe, "What do you think of my idea," he said.

"Great idea, Boss."

"So, first we find out where Pike went," Paz said. "Peggy, take Jack and go find out where Pike went."

Peggy wasn't happy about that. "Shit, Boss. Why me?"

Paz looked at him. He didn't say a word, just a steady gaze.

"Shit," Peggy said under his breath, struggling to his feet.

I followed him out. It was hot outside. The inside of the car was hotter. Peggy fired the vehicle up and turned the air on high. Peggy's vehicle was a Chevy Tahoe. He pulled out of the parking lot and I asked him to drive by the boarding house. He looked at me. I said "Really, I need to stop."

I gave him directions and he turned toward the boarding house. A couple of minutes later he pulled to the curb and I jumped out.

"Be right back," I said.

A minute later I was back carrying my crutches. I'd also shoved the Kahr in the back of my belt.

When I put the crutches in the back-seat Peggy said, "What are them for. I didn't think you needed them no more."

I climbed in front and he pulled away from the curb. "My disguise," I said. "Pike and his guys all know what you and the rest of the guys look like. I'll bet they don't know me. And, no one pays attention to a cripple on crutches with one foot. I can get closer."

Peggy was nodding, "Yeah."

He drove another couple of blocks, then said, "You ain't as dumb as you look."

"Why, Peggy, you'll turn my head."

He glanced at me, "What's that mean?"

I shook my head, "Nothing. It don't mean nothing."

"Just watch what you say, I don't take no lip."

"Yes sir."

Forty minutes later we were two blocks from Pike's place. Peggy had pulled into a lot and parked. I got out. I took my foot off and gathered up the crutches.

"I'll be back," I said, needlessly.

He didn't say anything. I started down the sidewalk.

I went to the bus stop in front of Pike's. I sat there like I was waiting on the bus. There was no one. No cars, no activity. Finally, I wandered around back on the pretense of checking the garbage bins. The stucco at the back of the place was chewed up by the automatic fire. The security lights were dangling. There were marks on the metal door. Other than that, there was nothing. Even the large garbage bins were empty. Of course, they could have been emptied this morning. I didn't know the garbage schedule.

I hobbled back to Peggy.

I put the foot back on, the crutches in the back, and slid into the passenger seat.

"Nobody home," I said.

He put the Tahoe in gear and pulled out on the street. He didn't turn back toward the freeway.

"Where to?" I asked.

"Mr. Paz says go find them, we go find them."

"You know where?"

"I know people that know where," he said.

I grinned at him. "Yeah, we find one of his dealers. They're going to know where to take the money. Hey, Peggy, you ain't as dumb as you look."

He didn't look at me, "I told you I don't take no lip," he said.

29

I was sitting in the Mustang about a half mile down Scottsdale Road from the night club district with Nacho beside me. My phone rang. I dug it from my pocket. I was expecting a call but I didn't recognize this number. I figured it to be a blind robo call. I connected and said "Yeah."

"Jackson? Is this Jackson?"

I recognized the voice. "Father Correa, as I live and breathe."

"How are you son? I haven't heard from you in a while."

"I'm fine, Father. Just chugging right along. What's up?"

"Well, I thought I better call you. Our friend has flown the coop."

"Reggie?"

"She was doing so well. Everyone liked her. Her quirky little personality. She loved playing with the babies. I had such high hopes."

"What happened?"

He was silent a moment. "I should have been more vigilant. One of the downtown churches brought a new one to me. We searched her clothes like we always do. We didn't find a thing. I had so much faith in Reggie, and we are so full, I bunked her in with Reggie. This morning I found the new girl stoned and incoherent and Reggie was gone. The new girl must have smuggled some crack or heroin in. I waited for Reggie to come back, but I'm afraid she probably won't."

"It's not a prison," I said.

"No, they are free to come and go as they please, I just had such high hopes."

I don't know why, but this wasn't a shock to me.

"I'll keep an eye out for her."

"Are you still acting out your little charade?"

"I'm still Jack Summers. I'd prefer no one knows we know each other. Quite frankly, it's safer for you that way."

"Do you still have your Apache angel looking over you."

"There is not an ounce of proof that Blackhawk has a drop of Native American blood in his veins, Apache or otherwise."

He laughed, "Every man should have the chance to be whatever he wants to be. If you see the girl, try to get her to come back. We were making such good progress."

"I'll do what I can," I said. He disconnected.

Nacho looked at me, "Who's Reggie?"

I grimaced, "Girl I was trying to help."

He leaned back and just looked at me. "Bring Jackson your poor, your huddled, your strung out and doped-up masses," he said with a grin.

I looked at him, "That almost sounded educated."

"Three years on the inside. I took history classes."

The phone rang again. It was Pete.

"Hey Pete."

"He's gone inside the club."

"We're on our way. Give us five minutes, then come in behind us." I disconnected. I pulled out into traffic and made my way to the club. We had to park two blocks away. The doorman stamped our hands after we paid the fee. He gave Nacho a long look.

Pete had said that Tommy always tried to get a table toward the back, as far from the dance floor as possible, so he could study the crowd. I spotted him. He was alone at a table for two. Behind him, and along the wall, was a bench upholstered in red vinyl. It was close enough, and it was empty. Without glancing at him I walked to the back and sat on the bench. I could have reached out and touched him. Everyone turned to look as Nacho followed me through the crowd. Here was a very big guy with long black hair. His shoulders were massive but his waist was small. He wore a wife-beater tee shirt that showed off bulging biceps covered with tattoos. And, to add to the dichotomy, he was carrying a briefcase. The music was pulsating as Nacho moved beside me and set the briefcase on the table in front of me. He leaned against the wall. Just far enough away to not be with me, but obviously there because I was. He made a point of studying everyone close by, just like a good bodyguard would.

A few minutes later a waitress came by. I ordered Johnnie Blue on the rocks. She looked at Nacho. He shook his head.

Our boy Tommy never turned to show any interest in me, but I know he was aware of Nacho, and therefore aware of me.

Right on time Pete came through the door. This was the tricky part. I had to be close enough to Tommy for Tommy to be able to make out our conversation. And, we had to do it before he got interested in a girl.

Pete did good. He wore a suit that was too big, his hair was slicked back with a heavy part, and a pair of really nerdy glasses was perched on his nose. He sat next to me on the bench, close to Tommy. This meant I would have to turn and lean forward to talk with him, thus projecting our conversation to Tommy.

"I didn't think you would be here."

"Why would you think that?" I said.

"After I gave you the money, I didn't think I'd ever see you again."

I saw Tommy shift imperceptibly, to be able to hear better.

"I told you this is legit. This ain't no scam. This guy's machine really works."

"Did it work?"

I turned and looked at Nacho. He leaned down and popped the briefcase open. He withdrew a manila envelope. He handed it to me. I handed it to Pete. Again Tommy shifted ever so slightly. Seemingly for a better look at the dance floor. But, now he could watch us out of his peripheral vision. Pete opened the envelope and reached in. He pulled out a large stack of bills.

"Holy, shit! How much is this?"

"It's what I told you," I said testily. "It's four times your money. That's the going rate."

"Four grand?"

"Five grand, counting your initial investment. You can count it if you wish, but you do that here, I can't guarantee what happens to you once you step outside."

Pete made a show of looking around. He stuffed the money back into the envelope.

The waitress came by, and I pointed at my empty glass. Pete shook his head. She looked at Nacho, but he was watching the crowd. She moved away. Tommy's drink was still full.

"I still don't get why you need my money?" Pete said on cue. "Why don't you do this yourself?"

I leaned back and drained my drink, the ice clinking against my teeth. The waitress brought the second drink and we were silent until she had moved away. I said, "The answer is simple. I don't have enough money for the guys to make me a partner." I leaned toward him, "Here's what I figure. I figure you will give me back the five large that's in the envelope and let me quadruple that. You see, you quadruple your money, but I take a large cut off the top. So far, this thing produces a lot more money than quadruple. Once I get a hundred G's we're done. That's the price tag they've given me. Then I buy into the business myself."

"How come no one else knows about this machine?"

I took a drink, "What my guy says is that people have been trying for a hundred years, but nobody figured it out till him."

Pete pushed the glasses back up his nose, "I want to meet this guy."

"No, you don't." I turned to look at Nacho. "You see this big guy?"

Pete leaned forward to look past me.

"This guy doesn't work for me. The man with the machine works for a bunch of guys. An organization. The big guy works for them."

"What kind of organization? Like the Mafia or something?"

"Make the Mafia look like Cub Scouts. These are guys that would chew me up and spit me out if I got sideways. They are letting me buy in because I did them a favor."

"What kind of favor?"

"You ask too many questions. Let's just say I'm an accountant. A damn good accountant." I held my hand out, "You back in? Or, are you out?"

He studied me just long enough. He handed me the manila envelope. I handed it to Nacho and he placed it in the briefcase. I looked at Pete, "You leave first," I said.

He stood without a word and worked his way through the crowd and out the door. I tossed a hundred-dollar bill on the table and stood. Nacho followed me out. As I turned to go through the door, past the bouncer, I glanced back. Tommy was watching us.

30

The first thing Paz hit was one of Pike's meth houses. He was pretty smart about it. The house was located far enough north of Baseline that it butted up against what Paz considered his territory. This would be a message.

Everyone but Frank and Paz turned out for it. Even Vanilla came along. The house was in an ordinary neighborhood, for that area. Run down, no landscaping. Three older model sedans and two pickup trucks were parked in the drive and along the front. It faced south. The house on the west side looked empty. There were broken children's toys in the dirt yard of the house to the east. No one was on the street.

Little Joe had briefed us on the way over. The house was used for manufacturing, but Pike also had his people sell out of it. It would be an easy hit Little Joe said. Peggy was driving, with Little Joe in the passenger side and the rest of us crammed into the back. Little Joe had given me a Smith and Wesson .38 with a three-inch barrel. I had crammed it into my back pocket and now was sitting on it. Like sitting on a rock. We were at 38th Avenue and Peggy was hot dogging. He came around the corner by the house fast enough to throw us on top of each other. Wally Chen was next to the door, so he bore the brunt of it.

"Jesus, Peggy. Take it easy," he growled.

Peggy turned the wheel and hopped the curb, pulling to a dusty stop in the yard. Little Joe gave him a hard look, but Peggy was grinning. He was enjoying himself. We all piled out. For a brief moment we stood looking around. Peggy turned and bounded up the steps onto the faded porch. He kicked the door in and went through it. We followed, Vanilla taking up the rear.

The room was a small living room. It had two really worn couches and some folding chairs. Two people sat on one of the couches. A man and a woman. They both looked strung out. Gaunt, emaciated, skin and bones. Covered in tattoo's. They didn't even react when we burst through the door. The place had the unmistakable odor of meth. Little Joe moved through the room to the back of the house. I followed him. We heard a back door slam as we moved into the kitchen. Bottles, tubes, a propane bottle and several boxes of matches were scattered about. I moved to a window just in time to see a guy going over the slat fence at the back of the scrub yard.

There were cans of brake cleaner and engine starter next to bottles of rubbing alcohol. The stove burners were still on. I absently turned them off.

"Turn them back on," Little Joe said. I looked at him. He was looking at the propane bottle.

"Hey," I said. "There are kids next door."

"Get everyone out of here," he said, like he hadn't heard me. He reached over and turned the burners back on, then moved to the propane bottle.

"Shit," I said under my breath. I went back into the living room. Peggy was rousting the guy. He had him up and was shoving him against the wall. Wally Chen was watching me.

"We have to get out. Little Joe's going to blow this place up."

Peggy was slapping the guy, backhand, forehand, like a punching bag. I reached down and grabbed the skinny arm of the girl. "Come on," I said. "We have to get out of here."

I shoved the girl toward the front door and turned and grabbed Peggy's arm. He spun, his eyes narrowed, his blood up. He reached for me. I turned his grasp aside and stepped back. "We have to get out!" I said. "Joe's got the propane open and the burner is on." He hesitated, staring at me, then turned and went out the door. Wally Chen pushed the druggie out after him. Vanilla was already standing out in the street. Little Joe came rushing out the door behind us. Peggy had jumped into the car and was backing into the street, tires spinning, throwing dirt up in clouds. We all started running. The girl was just standing there, so I grabbed her arm and pulled her along.

"My purse," she wailed. I drug her along. A half a block down, I let go and she staggered over and sat hard on a patch of grass. The guy had disappeared.

We stood watching the house. It took longer than you would think. Just when we were thinking that something had gone wrong the explosion took the back wall out. The concussion washed over us, then black smoke began billowing out of the back of the house. Peggy came screeching up to us in reverse. We piled in. The woman had disappeared. Peggy peeled away and even Wally Chen was grinning.

Little Joe pulled his phone and dialed 911. "I'd like to report a house fire," he said. Peggy laughed so hard he snorted.

31

Two days later Little Joe paid me my weekly grand. Two days after that I started driving the Mustang. Frank and Little Joe came out and admired it.

Little Joe slowly walked around it. Frank slowly pushed on the fender like he was checking the suspension. It must be a guy thing.

"So, you make a little money you get spick rich," Little Joe said. "Can't wait to spend it."

"Tired of walking," I said. "Makes my stub hurt."

"Nothing worse than a hurting stub," Little Joe said. Frank grinned.

"Har, har," I said.

One interesting thing was that Paz didn't expect me to hang out with the guys all day and all night. So, I didn't alter my routine that much. I came in and hung out till they closed up. I took to parking in the back. Since the firebombing, Frank had finally replaced the lights on the roof corners in the back. They didn't last long. One had already been blown out by a kid with a BB gun. I began parking the Mustang in the corner next to the row of oleanders. This is where Boyce startled me when she stepped out of the dark bushes.

"They found a body," she said.

"Well, hell," I said, stepping back. "Hello to you too. How you doing. How's the bag lady gig going?"

"That burned out house down off of Baseline. That was you guys." It didn't sound like a question.

"Paz sending a message. What body?"

"A woman. Not much left."

I looked off at the street, then around the area. It was dark and the street lights were lonely. I felt tired. I looked back at Boyce. The last remaining corner light threw a shadow of an oleander branch across her face. The shadow moved slowly in the light breeze.

"Tattoo's?"

She shrugged. "Don't know. Haven't seen the coroner's report."

"Where in the house did they find her?"

"She was in the front. Laying on her purse. Purse full of meth. Mendoza's getting impatient. Can we tag the woman on Paz?"

"Paz is too smart for that. He wasn't there."

"Were you there?"

I shook my head. "Nope, I ain't playing. They put you on the stand, you're an officer of the law. You are duty bound to spill everything. Nope, ain't playing."

She gave me that lopsided grin that looked sinister in the ambient light. "Don't you trust me?"

"Hell yes. I trust you. I trust you to be you."

"Everybody has to be somebody. You guys find out where Pike went?"

"Peggy shook it out of one of Pike's guys."

"Off of University and 24th."

I smiled. "Yeah. So, I just could have asked you?"

"We watched them move out of the old place, and we watched them move into the new."

"New place is like a fortress. Seven-foot block fence with a gate."

"You must have scared them."

"Something about Paz scares everyone. Even Peggy's afraid of him and Peggy's a psycho."

"Yes, he is. That's why Paz hired him. All Paz has to do is point his finger, and Peggy will chop your feet off."

"I'd like to have known his mother," I said.

"Probably Lizzy Borden. But none of Paz's guys are what you would call mentally stable. You look at Little Joe. He seems the most normal of the bunch. You check his rap sheet, you find that he was suspected of busting a guy's legs up by repeatedly dropping concrete blocks on them."

"Suspected?"

"Yeah. No arrest made, but he did it. And, he did it because Paz told him too. You can bet he has no regrets about it. Just another day at the office."

"Gee, and I like him too."

"Yeah, up till he shoots your balls off."

"What about Wally Chen?"

"Chen came out of Chinatown in San Francisco. We

think he got sideways with one of the Tongs; found the climate better in Phoenix."

"You know what's funny?"

"What?"

"I don't smell you. You think I'm getting used to it?"

She smiled. "I have. I guess you get used to anything."

"Mrs. Haggerty at the boarding house has a book of old tin type photos of early Phoenix settlers. Everyone dressed so proper, with hats and coats and some even with those little string ties."

She shook her head, "I'm sure this is a very important subject of conversation."

"This was way before air conditioning. Way before most things we take for granted. And, I was thinking about how they must have smelled. Not enough water to bathe every day. Washing clothes was really a chore. The heat was a killer. The body odor had to stink to high heaven, but they must have gotten used to it."

"Lots of cologne. They used lots of cologne. The only thing fancy about them fancy ladies was four layers of perfume."

"How long are we pulling this charade?"

"Up to you," she said. "You're the tactician."

"Yeah, well, I thought that if Paz got comfortable with me, we could catch him with his pants down. But, I can't find him with his pants down. We have to come up with something that will work."

"What will work?"

"We have to draw him out."

"How are you going to do that?"

"Hell, Boyce. I don't know."

She looked over my shoulder, then abruptly stepped back into the shadows. Then was gone.

I turned as I heard the footsteps in the parking lot. Peggy's shaved head gleamed in the light. I hit the remote to the car and it beeped as it locked again. I started across the lot toward him.

"Who you talking to?"

I walked past him, "Nobody."

He turned and fell in beside me, "The hell you say. I heard you."

I stopped and looked at him, "It was a panhandler, and she has a big crush on you."

He cocked his head, "Hey, I told you not to fuck with me."

I shrugged and started toward the door, he grabbed my arm. I stopped and looked at him.

"Paz wants to see us."

I looked at his hand on my arm. He dropped it.

"Lead the way," I said. I followed him in.

32

The meeting didn't last long.

Paz said to Little Joe, "Take Peggy and Jack and go find one of Pike's guys and take him to the river bottom and cap him."

"Which guy?" Little Joe asked.

"Doesn't matter," Paz said. "Just so the guy's important enough to Pike to matter. You know what I mean? And, leave him where he'll be found."

"Gotcha boss," Little Joe said. He was silent a moment, then "It's kinda late right now, boss. None of them guys might be out."

"Hell, yes it's late," Paz said. "Do it tomorrow night." He stood up and began shoving things into his briefcase." He could have been a mortgage banker. "Close this place up," he said. Little Joe and Wally Chen followed him out. I looked at Peggy, but he was struggling up out of the deep chair. He went by me without a look. I followed him into the bar. Peggy walked straight across and out the front door.

Frank looked at me, "We closing?"

I nodded, and went out. By the time I was in the Mustang, they were gone.

I didn't like parking the Mustang in front of the boarding house, so I still parked it in the parking garage and walked the few blocks back to my room. I went up the back stairs and the door to my room was unlocked. I pushed it open with my foot, my hand on the .38 in my back pocket.

Reggie was sitting cross-legged on my bed. She looked like hell, which is to say, I'd never seen her look better. She had gained weight, and while her hair was a mess, she didn't have that deep-down grime she had before.

I dropped my shirt tail over the handle of the pistol.

"What are you doing here?"

"Ain't you glad to see me?"

"No Reggie, I'm not."

I stepped in and closed the door quietly behind me. Habit.

"How'd you get in here?"

She grinned up at me. She seemed sober. "One of those old ladies let me in."

"They just let you in?"

"Sure."

"No, they didn't," I said. I picked up the bottle of lotion from my dresser and sat on the edge of the bed, as far from her as possible. I took off the prosthetic and began to work the lotion into my stump.

"I told them I had an important message for you, from your boss."

"What is it?" I asked.

Her grin got bigger, "Jack, there ain't no message."

I put the cap on the lotion bottle and set it back on the dresser. "Why are you here? Why did you leave Safehouse?"

"There ain't no rule I gotta stay there."

"No there's not. No rule. But, Christ Reggie. It's a place to clean yourself up, change your life."

"I don't want to change my life."

"Spoken like a true addict."

"I ain't no addict."

I didn't have to respond to that. "Why did you leave. Father Correa said you were making great progress."

"Progress? What the hell is that. You wake up in the morning and that's the best you will feel all day?"

"He said you did great with the babies."

She smiled. She almost looked human. "Yeah, there were some cute babies. This one named Raphael was so fat. You poke him with your finger and he would fall over laughing."

"Why did you leave?"

"Because, I wanted to. What's the deal with that guy anyway?"

"Father Correa?"

"Yeah father. Why do they call him father? He ain't nobodys father."

"He's a Catholic priest. They call Catholic priests Father."

She got off the bed and wandered over to the closet. She absently opened the door and looked in. "Why's that guy doing that anyway? How much money does he make?" She closed the door and looked back at me. "I'd charge a lot of money to put up with some of those bitches. The worse they were, the more time he spent with them. Some of them I'd just kick the hell out."

I felt this was probably useless, but I said it anyway, "Safehouse is a non-profit organization. Father Correa started it to help young women, especially pregnant young women, or young women with small children, that are being abused or have no place to go. Non-profit means the Father doesn't get paid. They exist on donations from other people."

"No shit? People just give him money?"

"Yes."

She cocked her head, looking at me. "I ain't pregnant. I don't have children. Why did he let me in?"

"It was a favor to me," I said.

"Why does he owe you a favor?"

"It's a long story. Listen Reggie, I can take you back to Father Correa's or you can leave, but you aren't staying here."

"You got anything to eat, Jack?"

"No, I don't, and I'm not going to get you anything to eat. You see, you think about it. The last time you ate something was probably out of a dumpster. The last good meal you had was at Safehouse. Life is nothing but a series of choices. We don't always get what we want to choose from, but we do get to choose. This is my last offer. I take you to Safehouse, or I walk you down the stairs and put you outside like a cat." While I was talking I slipped my prosthetic back on.

"Fuck you, Jack," she said, heading for the door.

I caught her by the arm. She started to pull away but realized she couldn't so she just stood there, her head down.

"You think I'll just let you leave so you can go downstairs and raid Mrs. Haggerty's refrigerator and sleep on her couch?"

Now, she tried to pull away. I just held her arm, tight. She was so skinny, it almost broke your heart. Almost. I opened the door and pulled her to the stairs and down to the outside door. I levered the dead-bolt open and shoved her out on the landing.

She turned, her face upturned, "Please, Jack."

I shut the door and locked it. I went up the stairs. She started pounding on the door and wailing. I waited in the hallway outside my door. It was as if everyone in the building knew what the noise was, and why. No one came out to investigate. After a while she was quiet.

I went in, locked the door, stripped down and climbed into bed. After a very long time I fell asleep. It wasn't just Reggie that had kept me awake, it also was the thought that I was supposed to kill a man tomorrow. And, this time it wasn't for God and Country.

33

Reggie was gone in the morning. I spent the day in my room reading and listening to NPR radio until I couldn't take it anymore. I shook my head at the antics of our political leaders. Not one of them would make it in the real world.

Finally, I showered, ate something and drove to the SanDune. When I walked in Frank said, "They're in the back. They're waiting for you."

"I didn't know I was supposed to be here at a certain time."

"You weren't," Frank said, wiping down a glass. "If you got here an hour ago, or an hour from now, they'd still be waiting for you."

I went into the back office. Peggy and Wally Chen were sitting on the couch. Little Joe was in the big chair. Vanilla was on a folding chair. Paz was behind his desk.

"Where you been?" Paz said.

I pulled my phone from my pocket and looked at it, "I don't have any missed calls," I said.

Paz looked at Vanilla, "Give him the chair," Paz said.

Vanilla's hairless eyebrows went up. He started to protest, but Paz's steady gaze held him. He reluctantly rose to his feet.

"I can stand," I said.

Vanilla moved to the back wall and leaned against it.

Paz waved a hand at the chair, "Sit."

I glanced at Little Joe. He was studying a fingernail. I sat.

"I been thinking about this," Paz said. "I've changed my mind. We ain't going to hit nobody. What we are going to do is grab Pike, take him to the river bottom and let him go."

"Let him go?" Peggy said.

Little Joe and Wally Chen were looking at Paz like nothing he said could surprise them.

"Yeah, let him go," Paz said. He looked at me, "Why would we let him go?"

All eyes shifted to me.

"Show him you can take him whenever you want. He'll be ready to deal."

Paz leaned back in his chair with a squeak.

"You're a smart kid," he said.

"How you gonna get him out of that gated compound he's in now?" Little Joe asked.

Paz looked at me, "How we gonna do that?"

I shrugged. "I don't know."

"You'll think of something," Paz said. He waved a hand, "Okay, everyone out for now, till Jack comes up with a plan."

We filed out and I went and sat on my usual stool. Little Joe moved up beside me.

"I told you not to get too cute with him."

"I have a terrible habit."

"What's that?"

"Someone asks me a question, I think they really want an answer."

"Yeah, you need to get over that," he said. He slid off the stool and went back to his normal table.

Frank set a beer in front of me, and I sipped on it for about an hour. Most of the time if I need an idea I just have to let it come. So, I sat quietly and looked at nothing in the mirror. After a while Peggy went out to smoke. When he came back in I had swung around to face him. The smell of cigarettes was pungent on him as he started to move by me.

He looked at me, "Got any ideas yet?"

"Who is Pike's largest income generator?"

He stopped. "Income generator?"

"Which of his guys make him the most money?"

He stood and looked at me. He was thinking. I could see that it hurt.

Finally, he said, "Probably Diego Luz."

"Diego Luz," I repeated. "Where does he operate?"

"He sells Pike's meth to all the chili pickers west of here."

"Where west?"

"Way west. Blythe and Quartzite, even on to Indio. We don't go there, so he doesn't have any serious competition."

"What's the most popular drug there. What makes the most money."

"OxyContin, hands down."

"Where do we find Diego Luz?'

"He works out of a ranch he has, out in Wintersburg."

"Where the hell is Wintersburg?"

"Way the hell and gone. West of Buckeye, south of the I-10. Gives him a straight shot to Blythe."

"You been there?"

"Hell, no. Why would I be out there?"

"You seem to know a lot about him."

"Paz keeps track of everything. That's why he's the King."

"But, Luz is working for Pike."

"If Cicero Paz wanted Diego Luz, Luz would be his."

"Why doesn't Paz go east? Into Scottsdale."

"Bunch of snots." Peggy snorted. "Nobody over there tough enough. Nobody wants to get their hands dirty."

"You got to get your hands dirty, huh?"

"You have to get your hands bloody," Peggy said, turning away from me.

34

The next day Peggy and I drove to Wintersburg. I had told Paz my idea, and with the wave of a hand, he said "Do it." Peggy insisted he knew where Luz's ranch was, and also insisted that Luz was alone, except for his 'woman'.

It wasn't just next door. We went west to I-17 then south to I-10 then just kept driving west. What used to be scrub desert and farms was now new developments designed like small towns. You never had to leave. But after a while we ran out of those also. We came to the Wintersburg exit and took it south. There just wasn't much out here. Peggy finally turned off the asphalt road onto a scraped dirt one. The dust boiled behind us. He drove another fifteen minutes then pulled to the side and shut off the motor. There was a gated drive just ahead. The gate was open, the drive was dirt. It wound five hundred yards back toward a dry knoll with a grouping of buildings on it. To the side was a barn and a large corral. In the distance, two horses lounged along the fence, munching on the sparse bunch grass. There was a pick-up truck by the house. There were two other buildings.

You couldn't tell their purpose. They could have been anything. There were four pick-ups by them. The truck by the house was the only one that looked half-way decent. The others were battered and rusty on the edges.

We sat studying the ranch.

"Thought you said he was alone."

"Usually is."

I looked at him, "How do you know?"

"Paz don't leave this guy hanging out here. He's got a guy inside, tells us what we want to know."

The buildings looked like they had been dropped from the sky into the middle of scrub, flat desert. There was hardly any growth. Some low creosote up on the knoll. Nothing around the buildings. When Peggy had said ranch, my mind went to cowboys and cattle and such. This was nothing but bare land.

"Diego Luz knows who you are?"

"Probably. He should."

"So, we walk up there, he knows you are from Paz."

"Probably."

"But, he'll probably want to know why you are here?"

"Probably."

"So, we draw him out, I put a gun on him, you zip tie him, and we drive him back to the city."

"What about those other guys."

"If they are there. I'll have a pistol to their boss's head."

Peggy looked at me. He studied me a minute. "What if there are guys there, and they start shooting."

"I have a gun to their boss's head. They start shooting, he's the first one to die."

His gaze was steady. I could see the questions in his eyes.

"We can turn around and go back," I said.

He started the car, "Little Joe says you have brass balls. We go back without Luz, neither one of us will have any balls."

We started down the long dirt drive to the house. There was a mongrel dog on the porch. It came to its feet, watching us approach. Diego Luz saved us the trouble. He stepped out on the porch, letting the screen door slam behind him. Peggy pulled the car up close to the porch and turned it so I was closest to Luz. He couldn't see Peggy. I had been wearing a ball cap. I took it off and put it in my right hand to cover the Smith and Wesson. I stepped out of the car. I walked up as close as I could before the dog started growling.

"Mr. Luz?" I said, with a smile. He was a big dark, rangy man with dusty black hair. He stood easy, his hands hanging at his side. They were as big as mitts. He had his share of Indio blood.

"Who wants to know?"

Peggy stepped out of the driver's side, and Luz started to move. With my left hand, I put the hat back on my head and with the right I pointed the pistol at Luz's middle. The dog was growling, but staying on the porch.

"Sic the dog and I shoot you first, then the dog," I said.

Luz moved his hands away from his sides.

"What do you want?" he said. He looked at Peggy, "I don't get into your business."

"Mr. Paz needs you to do him a favor," I said. "You have to come with us to the city to do it. Once it's done, you will be free to go. Mr. Paz will make it worth your while."

His eyes slid to the left and I stepped to the left so my peripheral vision could take in what he was looking at. Two men had come out of one of the buildings and were watching. Then two more came out. They carried AR15s.

"Peggy!" I said. Peggy moved around the car and up on the porch. The dog started to bark at him.

"Call the dog off, or I shoot it," I said.

"Loco," Luz said harshly. He held up a closed fist. "Bah!"

The dog shut up. It backed up a couple of steps with a whine.

Peggy pulled Luz's arms behind him. He had long zip ties attached to each other, making one long one. He wrapped them just above Luz's elbows and pulled them tight. Luz grunted. He took Luz by the arm and led him to the car. I walked along side, the pistol cocked and pointed at Luz's head. We went around the car so it blocked us from the four men. They were moving now. Peggy shoved Luz into the back seat. I got in the passenger's side, the pistol in Luz's face.

I heard the men shouting to each other.

"Time to go," I said.

"Shit," Peggy exclaimed.

I glanced at him, he was bent down in the driver's seat. Frantically retrieving the keys he had dropped.

By the time he had the key in the ignition, the men were on us. One on each corner pointing the automatic rifles at us.

"Get out of the car!" the man on my side shouted.

I leaned across the seat and grabbed Luz by his hair. I yanked him forward and shoved the pistol against his teeth. It split his lip and blood gushed down his chin.

"Open your mouth," I said.

He hesitated.

"Open now, or you die now," I said calmly.

He slowly opened his mouth and I shoved the barrel in. The hammer was back.

"Lower my window," I said.

Peggy hit the button and my window went down.

"If you shoot me, Luz dies," I shouted. "If you shoot the tires, Luz dies. If you shoot the driver, Luz dies. If one shot is fired, Luz dies. If I see a truck following, Luz dies!"

I said to Peggy, "Start forward, normal speed."

Peggy put the car in gear and we started rolling forward. At the last second the two men in front stepped aside. Peggy kept the car rolling. I watched through the back window until we reached the gate. None of the men had moved. With a jolt Peggy goosed the car and we took off in a boiling cloud of dust.

I pulled the barrel out of Luz's mouth. He spit a gob of blood on the floor board.

"Jesus," he said, and spit again. He looked at me. "Why do you do this? I stay out of Paz's business."

"This isn't about you," I said. "This is Paz and Pike."

His eyes just looked at me, dark and blank, as he processed this.

"How about you cut these damn zip locks? They hurt like hell. I will be no trouble."

I flipped my knife open and he leaned to the side so I could get to them. I sliced them. He leaned back rubbing his arms where they had bit into him. He looked out the side window, watching the desert go by. He stayed like that all the way back.

35

We were in Paz's office. Diego Luz sat in a chair, his elbows on his knees, his head in his huge hands. His dark hair hung over his hands and face. He looked up at Paz, shaking his head slowly, side to side. He took his hands and combed his hair back with his fingers.

"I do this, I'm done," he said.

"You don't do it, you're dead," Paz said.

Paz looked at Little Joe. "Put a gun to his head," he said.

Little Joe took out his pistol and put it to Luz's head. Luz didn't move.

Pax looked at Wally Chen. "Take a picture of that," he said.

Wally Chen stood and took his phone out. He moved around to get the right angle and took two pictures. He looked at Paz.

"You got your phone?" Paz asked Luz.

"I got it," Peggy said. He pulled Luz's phone out of his pocket. Paz nodded at Luz and Peggy handed him the phone.

"What's the number?"

Luz rattled it off.

"Send him the pictures," Paz said to Wally Chen. Wally Chen fooled with his phone a minute then Luz's phone pinged.

Paz held his hand out, "Let me see."

Luz handed him the phone. Paz looked at the pictures then handed the phone back to Luz. "You had no choice. We had a gun to your head."

Luz looked at the pictures then at Paz, "Pike won't care," he said.

"That's a chance I'll have to take," Paz said.

I smiled at that. Little Joe frowned at me and I stopped smiling. I guess Paz wasn't trying to be funny.

Paz looked at me, "You got what he's supposed to say?"

I took the typewritten sheet out of my pocket, unfolded it and handed it to Paz. He straightened it out and read it. He sat back looking at me, then at Luz, then he read it again. He nodded, "Yeah, that'll do it."

He said to Luz, "Call Pike, tell him what's on that paper. Don't read it, just say it. Make it sound normal. This is a deal too good to pass up. You try to get cute, Little Joe shoots you in the kneecap."

Luz took the paper and read it. He read it again. He looked up and this time he looked at me. He called Pike. The room was still. We could hear the tinny buzzing as Pike's phone rang. We heard him answer.

"It's me," Luz said. "Yeah, it's all good. Guy came over from L.A., he's got a deal for us." We could hear Pike say something. "Yeah, it's too big for me. I need you in it."

He listened a minute, then, "He has what he says is a million dollars of opioids. OxyContin, morphine, shit like that. He wants to unload them. Ten cents on the dollar."

He listened a moment, "I don't know. I don't want to know. The less we know the better. I've done business with this guy before. He's always delivered."

He listened again. "Cash, he wants cash. He wants to meet. He knows about you, he wants you in. He knows I can't handle it by myself. He says he'll bring samples and have photos of the whole thing." We could hear the sound of Pike's voice, but couldn't make out what he was saying.

"You decide," Luz said. "He said you decide, just so it's someplace private. Someplace he'll feel safe." He listened some more. "Where's that, again?" He listened. "Oh, your place. Your old place. It's still empty?" He was silent. "Tomorrow night, 8pm, your old place." He looked at the phone and disconnected. He looked at Paz. "You get that?"

"Smart," Paz said. "Nobody figures he would use that place again."

36

Because Pike had no idea who I was, I was chosen to be the dealer from California. Paz sent Little Joe, Wally Chen and Peggy to Pike's old warehouse five hours early. They took automatic rifles, and a deck of cards to pass the time.

At seven forty-five, I pulled into Pike's old parking lot and parked in the front. The sun was about done for the day and the automatic lights of the parking lot were buzzing as they struggled to ignite. Diego Luz was next to me. He was very quiet. Frank and Vanilla were in the back. Paz wanted a show of force. Once again, Paz wasn't going to dirty his hands and had stayed behind. I didn't see Little Joe's or Peggy's cars. I just had to assume they were inside, and they had gotten there before Pike's guys.

The Diamondbacks were playing a night game, so I found the broadcast and we sat in the gathering darkness listening to the ball game. This year they had a decent team. With them it was up and down.

Pike was right on time for Phoenix, which is to say he was fifteen minutes late. Pony Boy was driving. I knew that because the overhead lights glinted off his bald head as they turned into the lot. He angled the car so the lights were on us. I looked at Luz.

"Get out," I said. He reluctantly climbed out. Pony Boy looked at him for a long moment, then parked. He cut the lights. He stepped out, joined by three others. One of them was Bono Pike.

"This your guy?" Pike said to Diego Luz, his eyes on me.

"Yeah," Luz said.

He turned, "Let's go inside. I don't like standing in a spotlight."

Without looking to see if we followed, he walked across the lot to the front door of his old place. We followed. Pony Boy had the keys, he unlocked the door and we followed him inside. The place smelled musty. It was a reception area with an office off each side and a door to the back. Pike flicked the lights on. Someone was still paying the electricity. Pike turned to me, "Let's see what you got."

I made a show of looking around, "I want to make sure we are alone." With all of us in, the room was crowded.

He waved his permission and I went to the door to the back. I rattled the doorknob. If for some dumb reason the guys didn't know we were there, they would now. I opened it and looked through. When I turned back, Wally Chen followed with an automatic rifle covering the room. He was followed by Peggy, then Little Joe.

Pony Boy said "Shit," under his breath.

One of Pike's other guys started to move, but I had my pistol out and pointed it at him.

"Don't make a mistake."

"Where's the big guy, and the dude with the red bandanna," Peggy said. Pike looked at him, having no idea what he was talking about.

Peggy looked at me, "They ain't outside, are they?"

"Not with them," I said. "These guys all came together."

Wally Chen waved them against the wall and began patting them down. He was thorough, even checking their ankles. Peggy collected the weapons. Once they were clean, Wally Chen had them sit, facing the wall with their hands behind their heads. He saved Pike for last. Pike wasn't armed.

Little Joe pulled his phone and hit a speed dial number. The phone connected on the other end and Little Joe said, "It's clear."

A moment later the outside door opened and Paz walked in. He looked at the men sitting, facing the wall. He looked at Little Joe and nodded.

"Get up," he said to the men. The other men hesitated but Pike climbed to his feet. He showed no fear. He was a tall man, with gleaming boots and slicked back hair. His eyes were on Paz. He nonchalantly took a pack of cigarettes from his pocket and shook one out. He lit it and blew smoke out the side of his mouth, and upward, like he didn't want to blow smoke on anyone. It was the only outward tell that showed he might be nervous.

"You could have just called and asked for a meeting," Pike said.

"Would you have come?" Paz said.

"Probably not," Pike said.

"I could just kill you all now. Nobody would find you for a week."

Pike shrugged. "If you were going to kill me, I would be dead by now." He looked at Luz. "You in on this?"

Luz shook his head, but he did it with a certain amount of resignation, like he didn't think it would help much.

"I put a gun to his head," Paz said. "He didn't have a choice."

Pike took a drag on his cigarette, then waved it around the room. "Why go through all this?"

"So, you see I can take you anytime I want."

"So why not just take me?"

"I probably should, but you're a smart kid. I figure you can be more valuable alive instead of dead."

Pike dropped the cigarette on the floor and ground it out with a shiny, pointed boot. "So, you want me to work for you?"

Paz smiled. "No, that ain't your style. Not that you couldn't make a ton of money doing it. A helluva lot more than you are making now, but I figure you aren't a work for someone else kinda guy."

"You figure right," Pike said. "So, what's left?"

"I say a truce. A partnership, if you will."

Pike looked at him, the question in his eyes, "How does that work?"

"So, say we don't. We go to war instead. I blow the shit out of your places. You blow the shit out of my places. We start killing each other. We have to watch our back every living moment. My dealers get scared, your dealers get scared. Nobody wins. Nobody makes money."

"What's the answer?" Pike said.

"I've got an opportunity. It's an opportunity to go big. Really big. So big, I need to expand, and expand fast. I need more guys. More dealers, more soldiers. And, I need them now. So, I say we go partners," Pike started to say something, Paz held up his hand to stop him. "You keep your territory. You keep what you've got. You run it the way you want. I keep mine. But, we work together on this new stuff. We'll be twice as big, twice as strong. And, twice as big means quadruple the money. We can go further south, maybe even into Casa Grande and Florence. East into Mesa and Scottsdale. Maybe, even think about Tucson and Flag."

"What about Jose Flores and the Mexican's? Dione Lytel and his darkies, shit like that?"

Paz smiled. "They won't mess with us. Especially, us combined. They sell to their own people, mostly down the south part of town. That's the beauty of it. This new thing is all upper scale, Scottsdale, Mesa shit. Those dirt-bags won't mess with it."

Pike turned and looked at Pony Boy without seeing him. He was thinking about it. "How long to decide?" he finally said.

"Saturday," Paz said. "You got till Saturday, sundown. I don't hear from you by then, or you make any kind of move I don't like, I'll burn you down by Sunday morning." He looked at Little Joe and indicated the door with a cock of his head. Little Joe opened the door and Paz left. We all filed out, including Diego Luz. Guess he felt safer on this side than that. Peggy and Wally Chen were last. Peggy took their weapons and opened the inside door and threw them into the dark room. They hit the floor with a clatter. Wally Chen followed Peggy out, his AR-15 covering Pike and his men. Pike was lighting another cigarette. He was deep in thought. He didn't even glance up as we left.

37

I was trying to decide between Mendoza and Emil when Mendoza made my decision for me. I was sitting at the stop light where 7th Street, Cave Creek Road and Dunlap all converge when a patrol car came up behind me and lit up the lights. It gave the siren a short honk.

Looking in the rearview mirror I didn't recognize the patrol officer. I rolled the window down, put the car in park, and assumed the position. Hands at ten and two with my fingers spread. I waited. He took his time. Finally, he stepped out of the patrol car and came to my window, staying just far enough back to be safe.

"License and registration, Sir," he said.

I slowly pulled my wallet and slipped my license out. I handed him the license, lay the wallet in my lap and leaned forward to open the glove box. I was glad I didn't have anything in there but paperwork. I shuffled through the papers and found the registration. I handed it to him.

He looked hard at my license, then leaned down and looked hard at me. He looked at the license again, "Jack Summers?"

"Yes sir."

"Not Jackson? I was told your name is Jackson. No first or middle, just Jackson."

"Yes sir," Looking at him. What the hell?

"How do you explain that?" he said.

I gave him my most winning smile, "Your folks undoubtedly called you Bubba when you were little. But, it's probably not your name." I said.

He shook his head and handed me back the license and the registration. He hadn't looked at the registration. "The Captain said you were a smart ass. He wants you to follow me downtown. He wants to see you."

"Why didn't he just call?"

He turned without a reply, got in the patrol car, and with a wail of the siren pulled around me. I followed.

Mendoza wasn't in his office, so I went in and sat in one of the chairs. I put my feet up on the desk with my hands behind my head. Mendoza's office was three sides of plexiglass. The wall behind his desk was a normal wall with a window to the outside, as was befitting his rank. I could see across the room filled with desks for the detectives. Only three were at desks. I didn't recognize them. No one paid me any attention. A few minutes later, Mendoza came through the double doors that led down a hall. To where, I didn't know. He was carrying a folder. He came in and went around the desk, and sat down. He opened the folder and began reading. He hadn't looked at me. He was as crisp as usual. White, button-down shirt, blue tie. I'd noted the crease in his trousers, and the shine on his shoes when he had come in.

"Make yourself comfortable," he said, without looking up.

I recognize sarcasm when I hear it. I took my feet off of his desk and sat up. His office was spartan. There was a lamp on the desk, along with a computer monitor, keyboard and mouse. His only sign of humanity in the office was a framed picture of his wife, with his two girls, on top of the bookcase that held what looked like procedural binders. There were no papers, stacked or otherwise on the desk. Not a pencil, nor paperclip. His office was like he is. Neat, buttoned down, organized and functional.

After a long while, he closed the folder. He opened a drawer and searched for the exact spot the folder belonged, and put it away. Only now did he look at me.

"Any progress?"

I smiled. "You already know what I know. I think you know it about ten seconds after it happens."

"It takes a little longer," he said. "We had two bugs in Paz's place, but either someone found them, or they just died. So, we've been blacked out for a week." He turned the monitor so we could both see. He started typing. What looked like a grainy, black and white, video feed came up. "What can you tell me about this?"

I leaned forward to watch. I recognized Pike's parking lot. The view was from up high, like the camera was on a light pole, or in a tree. I watched as Diego Luz stepped out of our car. Then Pike and Pony Boy and his guys. Then me and Frank and Vanilla. We walked across the lot to the front door. A moment later we disappeared inside.

He reached over and fast forward the video. Paz went in that herky, jerky movement that fast forwarding does. We all came back out. Wally Chen had his Ar-15 pointed at the door until we were all in our cars and driving away. Diego Luz walked away until he was out of the picture.

"Where is he going?" Mendoza asked.

"Probably far away." I explained how I had gotten Pike to come out of his lair. Mendoza let me tell it without interruption. I left out how I had threatened to blow Luz's head off to escape his ranch.

"Whose idea was it to go back to Pike's old place?"

"Pike's" I said.

"Smart. I'm glad we still had the surveillance cameras up." He looked up at me, "When was the last time you saw Boyce?"

"The other night."

"And, you're not walking back and forth."

"Yeah, that too."

"Not so sure that was such a good idea."

I shrugged, "Walking got old. You try it with a prosthetic."

He leaned back in his chair. It squeaked. I was surprised he would allow it. "Boyce is having some trouble with some street kids."

"A gang?"

"No, not so much. Not like the Crips or Dos Hermanos. Just a bunch of kids that don't go to school, don't have jobs, sell a little dope, do a little dope. More of a nuisance than anything."

"What kind of trouble?"

"They just hassle her every time they see her. Rough her up sometimes."

I laughed. "Boyce can handle herself."

He nodded, "Bag lady's aren't supposed to handle themselves."

I thought about it. "What do you want me to do?"

"I send a squad car, they just disappear. I do it too often, they get suspicious. So, I thought maybe you could get them off her back."

"Consider it done."

He stood.

"Is that all?" I asked.

"Unless you have something else."

I stood, "Well, there is one thing."

"What's that?"

"I was wondering if, by chance, you had some gold dust I could borrow for a couple of days. Maybe in the evidence room. Just a small bag would do."

"Get out of here."

"No, really. I'm serious. Just a couple of days, then I'd bring it back."

"Gold dust?"

"Just a little bag. I don't need much."

"Get the hell out of here."

38

I found a convenient fire hydrant downtown, and parked the Mustang beside it. The Columbian Consul was in the same place, occupying half a floor in the high rise. The receptionist was still Rain. Beautiful girl, crisp white blouse bursting to perfection, short dark skirt. Sitting perkily behind the reception counter. She called herself Rain, but Emil said he thought her name was Gladys or something. I was surprised she was still here. The Ambassador's Attaché was Santiago Escalona. A good looking, suave and erudite man. While the Ambassador was in California, Escalona ran this office. He was a happily married man, and changed receptionists like other men change socks. It was usually because they began to believe they were special to him.

The Ambassador was heavily entrenched with the Valdez Cartel. Once upon a time, Blackhawk and I had wrenched the Ambassador's granddaughter from a bad situation. Emil had helped us. Emil was a huge, light-footed man, with a massive bald head on no neck at all. He was intelligent, educated, well read and well spoken. He was also the second most deadly man I knew. After Blackhawk. That was saying something, because in my former life I had known a lot of deadly men.

Rain looked up from her computer screen with her beautiful smile. I returned it with all the megawatt charm I could muster. This was the high wattage stuff that usually melted women's undergarments. She pretended not to recognize me.

"Hey, Rain," I said. "How's it goin'?"

Her smile didn't waver, "Do we know each other?"

"Oh, playing hard to get, huh?"

"Can I help you, sir?"

"How about you trot back and tell Emil his best friend is out here."

Now the smile faded a little, "I do not trot, sir. And, there is no one by that name here."

"Okay," I said. "That's the way we'll play it. Tell Emil I'll just be across the street getting a coffee." I turned and opened the heavy glass door. I stepped out, but before it shut I stuck my head back in. "We'll always have Paris."

Now, the smile had completely died. "I've never been to Paris," she deadpanned.

"Oh, how quickly they forget," I said, letting the door slide shut. She had already dismissed me, and was looking at her computer.

I had barely gotten set down with my coffee, in the Einstein Brothers across the street, when I saw Emil jaywalking through the traffic. If a car hit him, God help the car. He came in and sat across from me.

Without preliminaries he said, "All the way down here I wonder why in hell do I come down to see you."

"I'd see you up there, but Rain says you don't exist."

"She's right." He casually looked around the room, taking everything and everyone in. "I think I come down because you always entertain me."

"I aim's to please."

"Rain calls you, 'that guy that thinks he's God's gift to women'. I had to have her describe you before I realized who she was talking about. Do you think you are God's gift to women?"

I sipped my coffee. "Only if they are really old, and need help at a crosswalk."

"So, how can I help you find free money today?"

"I didn't ask the Ambassador for anything. And, your drug dealing friend made his own decision."

He smiled, "Yes, he did. It was to his own best interest. And, his excellency is a generous man. A grateful, generous man. And, that is mostly the reason I came down here. So, what brings you to my world today?"

I leaned back and looked at him. I thought of different ways to say it, but decided straight up was the best. "I need a bag of gold. More specifically, a bag of gold dust. It doesn't need to be a big bag, just so it is legitimate and the dust can be essayed."

Emil started laughing. He made a show of searching his pockets. Still laughing he said, "Wait, wait, I know I had it here someplace."

I shook my head, "I'm serious."

"I'm sure you are," he said. "Okay, you have to tell me the story."

So, I told him. I told him about Mrs. Eberly and the grifter, but I didn't tell him I was staying at the same boarding house, or why.

"So, this guy scams this little old lady out of her savings, and you want to scam him back with a bag of gold dust."

"Pretty much."

"Surely, there are other ways to scam the guy."

"Probably, but this one is so improbable I know he will bite."

"And, you think I have a bag of gold dust?"

I shrugged, "I think you know a whole lot of people, and I think you are a very resourceful man. So, I think if anyone I know could come up with a bag of gold, it would be you."

He studied me for a very long time. Finally, he shook his head and stood. "You are very entertaining," he said. He turned and walked out.

Several hours later, I was on the top deck of Tiger Lily with Pete Dunn. We each had a large rock glass with Plymouth gin and two ice cubes. We were watching the moon rise. Pete had been telling me how hard it was to sit before a blank screen and attempt to write the great American novel. That's why, I said, I was a reader not a writer. My phone vibrated. I pulled it from my pocket and looked at the screen. It said, "ID blocked". I started to disconnect, when I thought better of it, so I answered.

"Hello."

"I'm at the top of the hill," Emil's voice said. "I don't

want to come all the way down there, so you come up here."
He disconnected.

I stood.

"What's up?" Pete said.

I took a drink and set my glass aside. "Come with me," I said. "I want you to meet someone that no writer could make up."

It was our bad luck that the shuttle had quit for the night, so we hiked the two hundred yards, straight up, to the parking area. When we reached the top, I could feel the burn in my legs, telling me I had been neglecting my regular swims. Pete was huffing and puffing.

Emil was leaning, with arms crossed, against the passenger side fender of a dark limousine. The windows were tinted, but I could make out a guy in the driver's seat. In the moonlight, the light gleamed off of Emil's massive bald head. In his dark suit, his body looked like a tree in the black forest.

"Who's your friend?" Emil said.

"Pete Dunn," I said. "His boat is just down from mine. It used to be called the 'Moneypenny'. You may remember it."

Emil nodded. Pete held his hand out, "Nice to meet you," he said, struggling for breath.

Emil ignored the hand.

"Pete's a writer," I said.

"Nothing here to be written about," Emil said looking at me.

"Not a thing," Pete said. "Jackson said I should meet you. Said you were, uh, unusual."

Emil looked at me, then back to Pete, "He said *I* was unusual? The one-footed wrecking ball said *I* was unusual?"

Pete laughed. "Wrecking ball?"

Emil reached into his pocket and took out a small leather pouch. He handed it to me.

"There's three ounces of dust in there. You have three days. If I don't have it all back in three days, the catfish will feast on your toes."

"It might work better if you said, liver, or eyeballs," Pete said.

Emil looked at him, then back to me.

"Thanks," I said.

Emil looked at Pete again. He shook his head and got into the limo. The driver fired the engine, and it pulled away, grinding through the loose gravel.

We watched it drive away.

"Wow, you were right," Pete said. He looked at the pouch in my hand, "Is that it?"

I hefted it in my hand. It was a sold weight. "That's it," I said.

39

Blackhawk, Nacho and I were in Nacho's Jeep parked in the strip mall lot at Dunlap and 35th Avenue. On the corner, Boyce was in her bag lady regalia, holding a cardboard sign that said, *homeless hungry anything helps – God Bless.*

She was sitting with her forearms on her knees, her head on her forearms. She didn't really want anyone to give her anything, but once in a while someone did. We started keeping track. It seemed like it was usually younger women or older men. When they did give her money, she would stash it in a bag in the overloaded shopping cart she had sitting back, away from the street. I had asked her what she did with the money. She said she gave it to the patrolmen that drove her home every night. They dispersed it to other homeless in the area the next day.

We'd been there an hour when Blackhawk said, "Head's up."

I looked to where he was looking. A block away a group of boys came into sight, sauntering down the sidewalk, coming toward Boyce. They were young. Too old to just go out and play, too young to drive.

When they reached the corner, they surrounded Boyce's shopping cart and began to rummage through it. We could hear her screeching at them.

"We gonna just sit here?" Nacho said.

I nodded, "Yeah." He shrugged.

"Boyce is okay," Blackhawk said. "She can handle this."

One of them found her stash. She tried to grab it out of his hand, and he shoved her down. She stayed down. She did this to stay out of their way. No sense getting punched for someone else's money. She was screaming a string of invectives at them that would blister a wart hog.

Once they had her money, they lost interest in her. We watched them move on down the street. Boyce dusted herself off, and offered her cardboard sign to the current string of cars. Two drivers, who had witnessed her being bullied, offered her money.

The boys were a couple of blocks away when they turned a corner and moved out of sight.

"Follow them," I said to Nacho. He fired up the Jeep and pulled out into the street. He took his time getting to the corner. He pulled around it, and the boys were only a half block up. They were acting like young boys everywhere. Silly.

"I want to know where they go," I said.

Nacho pulled into the parking of a small furniture store. We sat and watched. Three blocks up they turned another corner. Nacho started the Jeep and we moved again. By the time we made the turn, they were half a block down. This time they turned into an auto repair shop. The asphalt parking lot was filled with older cars. The building was big enough to have two bays. They skirted the shop and went to a free-standing building that was a hundred feet behind the repair shop. They went inside. The building was small, maybe 600 square feet. It had a door with windows on each side. The windows were opaque, with years of grime. You couldn't see inside.

Nacho pulled into a vacant parking slot and looked at me.

"Let's go talk to them," I said.

"Kinda young to beat up," Blackhawk said.

"We just want to scare them off Boyce."

We started to get out, when we heard the thumping bass. Then we saw the SUV. It pulled into the lot behind us, passed us and parked by the building the boys had gone into. The speakers were pegged to the point of distorting. Heavy rap filled the air. Why is it that the people that like the worst music have to play it the loudest? Then, it abruptly stopped, and three men got out. They all were dressed gangster style. Ball caps on sideways, Cleveland Cavalier and L.A. Clipper jerseys and fluorescent bright basketball shoes. They were all big, one was huge. So huge the shocks on the car sang a chorus of Hallelujah when he got out.

"Jesus," Nacho muttered. We watched them go into the building.

"Those aren't boys," Blackhawk said.

"We gonna scare them off?" Nacho said.

"Nah," I said. "Not you and me."

He looked at me.

"Blackhawk will."

"You're hilarious," Blackhawk said.

I got out. I waited beside the Jeep. Waiting to hear doors open and close. Finally, I heard one. I waited, then I heard the other. Whew.

"Theirs not to make reply," I said. "Theirs not to reason why, theirs but to do or die. Into the valley of death, rode the six hundred."

"You are truly weird," Blackhawk said.

"I got a bad feeling about this," Nacho said, coming up beside me.

"Piece of cake," I said. I went to the rear of the Jeep and lifted the hatch. Inside was a sawed-off 12-gauge Mossberg. I handed it to Nacho. He pumped in a round. I took the .45 caliber Kahr from my back pocket and racked a round into the chamber. Blackhawk was holding a .357 caliber Smith and Wesson revolver next to his leg. He was watching me.

I nodded and we walked to the door. Without hesitation, I turned the knob and opened it. We went in, me moving left, Blackhawk moving right, Nacho right behind. It was all one big room, furnished for recreation. A huge flat screen TV at one end. A pool table in the middle, dart board on the side, and several easy chairs and couches. The guys were all sprawled around. Nacho blew the TV into pieces.

The great big guy was sunk into a couch. He jumped when the shotgun went off, then he began struggling up. Blackhawk took a step and smacked him upside the head with his pistol. He fell back, his weight almost tipping the couch. I had the room covered. Everyone froze.

I walked over to the kid that I had seen taking Boyce's money. I pointed the Kahr at his forehead. His eyes were wide with panic.

"Give me the bag lady's money," I said.

"Whaa?"

"You've been hassling that bag lady down on her corner. You took her money. It's in a green bag. Give it to me."

"Hey, man, you can have it," he said reaching under his chair. He handed me the bag. I shoved it into my back pocket. Nacho had the door open. I looked around, making eye contact with everyone in the room.

"Leave the lady alone," I said. "Anyone hassles her again, we'll be back and burn you down."

One of the kids said, "Hey, man. What's it to you? She's just a bum."

I looked at him until he got nervous. I nodded toward Nacho. "She's his sister. She's a doper and a bum, and she can't defend herself. But, she's still his sister."

Blackhawk backed to the door. "Anyone sticks his head out this door for the next five minutes, gets it shot off," he said. I went out and he followed with Nacho shutting the door behind us. Nacho kept the shotgun aimed at the door until we were in the Jeep. He handed the shotgun, butt first, to Blackhawk in the back seat, got in and started the motor.

"Why does she have to be my sister?" he asked.

"Family resemblance," Blackhawk said.

40

Nacho and I were outside the same club in Scottsdale, waiting for Pete to follow Edward/ Grover/Tommy into the place. I guess he would be Tommy tonight. Pete's job was to place himself where Tommy could see him, hoping Tommy would take the bait and start talking with him.

I was anxious to get on with this, so the time seemed to crawl. Finally, enough time passed and Nacho and I went into the club. Again, the noise was a wall, a din that seemed almost physical. We stepped to the side of the door and waited for our eyes to adjust. I saw Tommy against the back wall, in the same place as last time. Pete was close by, but they weren't together. Looks like I needed more bait to catch this fish.

Pete was watching for us, and waved for our attention. We made our way over. I sat next to Pete while Nacho moved a chair a little bit away from us. Pete and I leaned toward each other to be able to talk above the din.

"He knows I'm here," he said. "I caught him looking at me."

"I'm going to talk awhile, you act like you don't like what I'm saying." He nodded.

"I'm telling you that I don't have your money, and you are not happy. Get mad at me. I leaned back to Nacho. "When Pete starts yelling at me, you intervene. Grab his arm, or something." I leaned back to Pete, and told him again that I didn't have his money, but I had something better.

Pete played it well. Must be being around all those actors. He came to his feet and with both hands on the table, leaned into me. "You promised me you would quadruple my money," he shouted. Nacho stood and came around me, grabbing Pete. Pete tried to shake loose, but Nacho held him tight. Across the room, one of the security guys started toward us, then saw Nacho had Pete under control and stopped. He watched us, then turned and went back to his post.

I took the bag of gold dust out of my pocket. I held it up for Pete to see, but more importantly, for Tommy to see. Nacho released him and they both sat. I handed Pete the bag. He hefted it, then undid the tie string and looked inside.

"I'm told by the assayer that there is north of ten thousand in gold in there," I said.

"Ten? You promised me four times the investment," Pete said loudly. I glanced at Nacho and he greeted it with an imperceptible nod. Tommy was watching, and more importantly, listening.

"You got four times the first time. Now you get double.

There is no guarantee what the machine will pick up on any given run. This time it was ten. You double your money and you bitch."

Pete glared at me for a moment, hefting the bag in his hand. I nodded at Nacho, and we stood to leave.

Pete grabbed my arm. "Hey, what about again?" He proffered the bag to me. "Let's do it again."

I shook my head, shaking loose of him. "My partners are already pissed that I'm not bringing them real money. Even with the ten, that's not enough. You don't have enough. We're done."

"Ten's not enough?"

"You come back with fifty and we'll talk." I nodded at Nacho, and we stood and walked out. As we stepped outside, Nacho said, "He was listening to every word."

Two hours later Pete came into the main saloon of El Patron. I was at the corner stool and Nacho was across from me, reading a book. An honest to God book. The cover depicted a muscled bare-chested man, and a buxom woman, swooning into each other's arms. Pete was grinning. He sat next to me. Jimmy brought him a Dos Equis, to match mine.

"I have a new partner," he said.

"Do tell," I said.

"Yeah, he came over right after you left. He went straight to it. He said, 'Is what's in that bag, what I think it is?' I made a big show of looking around, like I was afraid of being robbed."

"So, you showed it to him?"

"Not at first. I made him practically beg. He was very charming. Very convincing. I could see why those women just handed their money over."

"But, you did show it to him?"

"Eventually. So, then he says he had overheard our conversation, and he had heard I didn't have enough money for an investment. He said he was a speculator and that for the right thing he would invest up to a hundred thousand dollars. So, he wanted me to explain what the investment was."

"Did he buy it?"

"Not at first. But, the gold dust was brilliant. I explained how your partners had a machine that dug up the tailings at old gold mines, and through centrifugal force separated out the gold that conventional methods left behind. He didn't believe it at first. Why hadn't someone done this before? The same arguments you told me he would have."

"What did you tell him?"

"What you told me to tell him. Centrifugal sifters had been around for years, but they all used the same kind of electrical motors, so they were never fast enough to separate the really tiny particles of gold that was left behind. I told him your guy invented a machine utilizing a jet engine motor, and the LI900 Silica Ceramic they use on the Space Shuttle that could withstand the speed and force of a much more powerful engine, and bingo. Out comes the gold. The kicker was when I showed him the gold in the bag."

I grinned at him. The Silica Ceramic was his idea, "And, he wanted some to test."

"Yep. He went to the bar and got a shot glass. He had me shake out what we thought to be a hundred dollars' worth. It wasn't much. He put it in an envelope, and gave me a C note. We agreed to meet in a week."

He took the bag from his jacket pocket and handed it to me. It pretty much weighed what it had before.

"Where's the C-note?"

"In the bag," he said.

I leaned back, sipping on the beer, looking across the room, thinking.

Nacho looked up, he had his finger holding his place on the page of his romance novel, "Hey, what does conjugate mean?"

41

Paz called a meeting for 6pm, Saturday. I got there early. Paz, Little Joe and Wally Chen were already there. They were in the bar instead of Paz's office. This was a first for me. Paz never hung out in the bar. There were no customers, Frank must have closed the bar and sent them all away. Peggy and Vanilla followed me in by two minutes. Paz sent Peggy back outside to stand by the door. Peggy checked his piece before he stepped outside.

"Get'm a drink," Paz said to Frank. Frank gathered glasses. I went behind the bar and got my own. He topped off everyone else's with Woodford's Reserve. The good stuff. There was a dusty bottle of Mr. Boston blended whiskey, I picked it up and poured a shot into my glass. I selected it because it had a screw top, but more importantly it was made of dark brown glass that hid the contents. As I put the lid back on, I dropped the dime sized, water proof, microphone into the bottle. I set the bottle back in its place, and turned, sipping the drink. No one was looking at me. They were used to me being behind the bar.

The clock behind the bar gave us ten minutes until 6. I didn't know if the meeting was to announce Pike accepting Paz's offer or a declaration of war. Either way, Mendoza wanted it recorded. I thought he already had this place wired but he had told me the equipment he had in place had failed. This microphone was, supposedly, state of the art. It insured everyone was heard and everyone was identified.

We sipped our whiskey and waited. No one else seemed nervous. When the big hand hit 12, Peggy stepped back inside the door.

"They're here," he said, his pistol in his hand.

"Put your piece away," Paz said. Peggy did it. He didn't like it, but he did it.

A moment later Pike and Pony Boy came in. Through the door I could see more of Pike's guys outside. They looked tough and competent.

Paz was sitting at the end stool. He slid off and came forward. He extended his hand to Pike. Pike took it.

"I'm glad you came to hear us out," Paz said. "Nobody wants a war."

"I'm not saying I'm in till I hear the particulars," Pike said. "I'm intrigued enough to listen."

Paz turned to Frank, "Gett'm a drink, Frank."

"What's your poison?" Frank said.

Pike looked behind the bar at the bottles. "Turkey on the rocks," he said. "Make it a double."

Frank deftly scooped ice into a rock glass and poured the drink. He looked at Pony Boy. "How about you?"

Pony Boy shook his head. "Nothing for me," he said.

"Maybe he wants a Shirley Temple," Peggy said.

Paz turned on him, "Shut your mouth. You open it again, I'll put my boot in it."

I couldn't help it. I looked down at Paz's feet. He was wearing shiny, black loafers. It must have been a metaphor.

Paz turned to Little Joe, "Put some tables together so we can all sit down." He looked at Pike, "I'd have you back to the office, but we can't all fit, and I want everyone in on this."

Pike raised his glass to show he agreed.

Little Joe and Peggy started sliding tables, and placing chairs until we had one long table surrounded by the chairs. Paz indicated a spot across from where he stood. "Why don't you set there," he said to Pike. Pike did. Paz sat across from him, strangely leaving the chair at the head of the table empty.

After we all were settled, Paz stood. "In a moment, a guy is going to join us. When he gets here, I will explain the deal." Pike frowned and glanced at Pony Boy. Pony Boy was watching Peggy.

The tone of this could have been a sales meeting in a corporate board room. Paz was right, a moment later the door opened, and a tall man stepped in. He was followed by a hawk faced man in an expensive suit. Hawk Face carried a briefcase and pulled a small, carry-on suitcase on rollers. The tall man wore a gray suit and I recognized him. He had been here before. Hawk Face was new.

The gray man strode across the bar like he owned it. Paz stood, and he and Paz shook hands. Paz indicated the chair at the head of the table and the gray man went to it and sat. Paz sat.

Paz said to the man, "You have the floor."

"The gray man said, "My name doesn't matter. If you need to have a name to help the discussion along, you can call me Mr. Stein. Before we get started we need to take care of a small formality. My associate," he turned and indicated Hawk Face, "will need to insure our privacy. This is in no way impugning the character of anyone here, but it will make us able to speak more freely."

While he was speaking, Hawk Face was opening the suitcase and extracting a machine. Attached to the machine was what looked like an electric wand. I recognized it immediately. TSA uses them at the airports.

Mr. Stein continued, "My associate will ask each of you to rise, in turn, and he will use his equipment to insure no one is wired." He turned and looked at Paz, then at Pike, "I'm afraid this will include you, Mr. Paz, and you, Mr. Pike."

Paz waved his hand in dismissal. Hawk Face started at my end and one by one we rose for him to move the wand around and up and down our entire bodies. He watched the monitor closely. I had the .38 special in my back pocket, and my pocket knife in the front. I had to reveal both. Neither seemed to bother him, or the gray man. Everyone had a piece they had to show, except the gray man and Paz, and maybe Hawk Face. He didn't check himself. Peggy had a problem with the gold chain around his neck. He also had a heavy gold bracelet, but Hawk Face was interested in the necklace.

He had to take it off for Hawk Face to examine. Once Hawk Face was satisfied, it was okay.

Finally, he turned to the gray man and said, "All clear."

"You can wait in the car," the gray man said. Hawk Face packed up his gear and left.

Now Mr. Stein looked at Paz and said, "Your show."

Paz looked around the room. "I've asked Mr. Stein here to work out the details of a new business proposition. You all know we are meth and cocaine, uh, advocates. It's a good business, but times are changing. The big money in American is in opioids. Mr. Stein's company distributes opioids to pain clinics all over the west." He turned to Mr. Stein, "How much does an opioid pill cost at a pain clinic?"

Mr. Stein said, "Four to five dollars."

"Four to five dollars," Paz repeated. He looked at Little Joe, "How much can you sell opioid pills for on the street?"

"Twenty-five to forty dollars apiece."

"You do the math," Paz said looking at the rest of us. He turned to Mr. Stein, "We've all heard about opioids, but even I don't know much of the technical stuff. Tell the boys about opioids."

Stein shrugged, "Opioids are a legitimate pain killer. Opioids like oxycodone, hydrocodone, methadone and fentanyl are prescribed every day. They are also highly addictive, and addicts will do almost anything to get their hands on them. And, you can't just cook them up like meth. For instance, oxycodone is made primarily from a semi-synthetic opiate. These are Schedule ll controlled substances. Heavily regulated, and hard to come by, unless through legitimate sources. Doctors and clinics all over America are getting rich prescribing these drugs. If they were available on the street, can you imagine the money involved?"

"Might as well be us," Paz said.

"You the supplier?" Pike said to Mr. Stein.

Stein looked at Paz, and Paz answered. "Out of all the clinics Mr. Stein's company has in the Valley, there are two that serve as their main distribution centers for the southwest. The pills are shipped in from the manufacturer, then those two supply the other clinics. Some of those shipments will end up, let us say, diverted."

"And no one will notice?" I asked.

Mr. Stein looked at me. "If my company opened a dozen more clinics, that would be noticed. Think about this. In Mohave County four doctors prescribed 6 million pills. That is not a big county. That's enough pills to medicate every citizen in the county four times a day for a week. This is a big business. Why should those guys get rich, and not us?"

"Where's Mohave County?" Wally Chen asked.

"Up around Kingman. A stone's throw from Vegas," I said.

"How much we gonna sell this stuff for?" Peggy asked.

"Mr. Stein, Mr. Pike and I will figure that out." Paz said this to Pike. When Pike looked at him, Paz said, "You in?"

Stein was surprised. "I thought this was settled."

Pike said, "It is." He nodded at Paz. "I'm in."

Paz stood. "Mr. Stein, why don't you and Mister Pike come back to my office?"

Stein stood. He and Pike followed Paz to the back. We all sat for a moment, looking at each other. Peggy began to grin.

Frank went behind the bar, "Bar's open," he said.

We all stood and moved to the bar to get a drink. Peggy stood next to Pony Boy. "We're all gonna get rich," he said.

42

I sent Nacho and Jimmy to the Scottsdale hook-up bar as bait for Tommy. The next afternoon I was in El Patron, at the bar, nursing a beer. Nacho was next to me, Blackhawk and Elena up in the apartment.

"So, he didn't waste any time," Nacho was saying. "As soon as Jimmy and I sat down he came over."

"So, he wants in, but he doesn't want Pete in."

"Exactly."

"What did you tell him?"

"I told him I'd relay the message. He offered $75.000. Trying to make himself irresistible. I told him if it was a deal, I'd be back tonight with you."

"He ask my name?"

"Yeah."

He was sipping a beer. He kept sipping.

"What did you tell him?" I finally said.

He turned to look at me. He was smiling. "I told him your name was Jackson and that you lived on a houseboat at Pleasant Harbor Marina."

My eyebrows went up, and he started laughing. He held a hand up to ward me off, "No, no, I told him your name was Smith."

"Jerk. What time tonight?"

"Nine."

I sipped my beer and thought about it.

I wanted Tommy to wait, so we didn't walk into the club until twenty after nine. He was back against the wall and stood when we came in. God, I was getting to hate this place. What the DJ considered music was just an obnoxious, shrill, thumping abasement to my ears.

Nacho nodded toward Tommy, and I followed him over. Tommy was studying me as I studied him. At last he put on his best sales smile and stuck his hand out. I ignored it.

"Check him," I said to Nacho.

Nacho lifted both his palms up to indicated to Tommy to raise his arms. Tommy frowned, and didn't move. Nacho stepped into him and lifted each arm away from his body, and began to frisk him. Tommy was startled, but he didn't resist.

Finally, Nacho was satisfied. "Clean," he said. Of course, he was. I'd have been shocked if he wasn't, but it was just another piece of theater to further Tommy's belief in who I was.

I waved Nacho away, and he took a spot along the wall, just out of earshot.

Tommy and I both sat with our backs to the wall. "I've been told you want to see me," I said.

He leaned forward, "I want in," he said.

"In?" I said. "You think that's it? You want something and it happens?"

"I have seventy-five thousand reasons why it should."

The waitress stopped. I ordered Johnnie Blue on the rocks. Tommy already had a drink in front of him, but it looked untouched. He was here for business.

I waited until the waitress brought the drink. "Those are compelling reasons," I said as she moved away. I took a drink. "The trouble is, you tell people here," I indicated the room with my drink. "That your name is Tommy. But, Tommy doesn't exist."

He shrugged. "It's as good a name as any."

"So, I had you checked out. The car you have parked outside is leased to Edward Burns, but that isn't your name either."

He leaned back and looked at me. "You a cop or something?"

I let out a genuine laugh. "No more than you are. But, I am connected. My associates have people everywhere. There are few secrets they can't uncover. I'm told your name is Grover Hilland. You are thirty-three years old, you were born in Dayton Ohio. You are not married and never have been, you have no children that can be found. In fact, you have no next of kin that can be found."

I thought, this guy could be me.

"The other pertinent thing we discovered is that you don't seem to be employed, but you live well. That makes us wonder."

"I'm a speculator. I see something that I think will turn a profit and I put money into it."

"And you think I will turn you a profit."

"Yeah, the gold thing. I still think it looks hokey, but that other guy, he had a bag of gold dust. Who has a bag of gold dust? I had it checked. It was real gold dust. He told me how he got it, but I want you to tell me, before I, huh, invest." He paused, frowning, "You know, I've haven't used the Hilland name for a long time. It makes me suspicious you can come up with it."

"I didn't." I nodded toward Nacho. "See that guy? He's not just here to keep me safe, he's also here to watch me. There's too much money in this for anyone to trust anyone. His bosses are the ones that dug into your past. And, believe me, they have the resources, local, state, federal."

"You said you don't have enough money to buy into it," he said.

I leaned back and looked at him. "Pete has a big mouth."

"Pete? That his name? No, it wasn't Pete. I overheard you talking to Pete. But, what I don't understand is if these guys are so well connected, what are they doing with you?"

I smiled, "Good question." I took another drink. "I was the one that found the Professor and his magic machine. I brought it to them. They let me stay close enough to get some of the scraps."

"How'd you find him?"

"I was, am, a geological engineer. I've been in mining my whole life. Since the beginning of mining, men have been trying to extract as much gold as possible from the earth. The interesting thing about gold is that it is not formed on this earth. You can say all gold is extra-terrestrial. All the gold on earth came from outer space."

"That don't make sense."

"No, it wouldn't. Not unless you have the education about it. But, it doesn't matter. What matters is that gold is heavy. The old miners took a gold pan and sluiced the gravel in the creek bed hoping for the gold to stay at the bottom. Modern day gold mines dig and there are machines that extract the gold from the rest. Engineers have always wondered how to get the most minute particle of gold out of the discarded tailings. No one ever found a way."

"Until now," he said.

That's when I knew I had him. "Until now," I repeated.

"This Professor figured it out?"

"He did. Up until now, no one had a machine that could spin fast enough to separate the tailings from the gold, without just burning up. I heard about this guy while I was in Nevada. He was just another crackpot, but there was something interesting enough about him to make me check him out."

"What was that?"

"He is an aeronautical engineer. He figured out how to use a jet engine and something called LI900 Silica Ceramic. And, it worked."

"Where is it?"

I drained my glass and signaled the waitress. I hitched around to look at him. "You seem like a smart guy. Probably as smart as me. I figured it out, so I'll bet you could too. The largest gold mine in America is in Nevada. That's where they found the Carlin Trend. There's seventeen open pits and four underground mines. All we had to do is get permission to sift through the tailings at one of the abandoned places."

"Do they know you are getting more gold out of it?"

The waitress brought my drink, and I dropped a fifty on her tray. She smiled at me and moved away. "Hell no. As far as they know, we are striking out just like all the other losers that have tried."

"How much have you got out of it so far?"

"You said it yourself, I don't have enough money. I'm getting the scraps. But, let's say you come up with a hundred grand. We double, triple, quadruple the money. I take the original hundred as my fee. You take the rest, reinvest half of it, I reinvest my hundred. As long as there are abandoned gold mines, the goose keeps laying the eggs."

"What's the Professor get out of it?"

I looked at Nacho. Tommy's eyes followed mine. "His life," I said matter-of-factly. "And, his family, with enough money to last the rest of his life."

He thought about it, "Hell, man. That's a lot of money."

"You talking about the hundred, or what you're going to get back?"

He finally took a drink. He was nodding.

43

It was late when I parked the Mustang and walked back to the boarding house. I was feeling good. Same as when you get that first big-fish strike, and you know he's on the hook. I went around to the rear entrance and had the key in the lock when I heard a noise. Behind me, in the oleanders. I didn't move. I made no sound and listened. I heard it again. It was a low moan. The street lights had ruined my night vision, so I stood and stared into the darkest part of the bushes, letting my eyes re-adjust.

On the third moan, I moved silently back down the steps, and moved into the grass to muffle my footsteps. Now, I could make out a small dark mass at the base of the bushes. I cautiously moved to it.

It was Reggie. She was curled into the fetal position. Her breathing was ragged and shallow. She was unconscious. I felt the pulse in her throat. It was slow and irregular. I fumbled my phone from my hip pocket, and hit Boyce's speed dial.

"What do you want?" her voice said.

"I've got an overdose in the bushes behind my boarding house. My car is five blocks away, and I need to get her to the emergency room. Is your patrol car still in the vicinity?"

"Yeah, they just picked me up. What's the address?"

I told her.

"We'll be there in two minutes."

It was less than that. They pulled up, their lights flashing. I activated my phone, so it lit up, and waved it at them. Boyce was still the bag lady. They all hustled over to me.

"Anyone got Naloxone?" I said.

"In the trunk," one of the cops said. He turned and ran back to the car. Reggie was struggling to breathe. The other cop and I rolled her to her side, hoping to clear the airway. The cop returned with what looked like nasal spray.

"All we have is the nasal inhaler," he said.

I rolled her back and put my arm behind her back and sat her up. The cop got the spray bottle into her nostril and squeezed. Nothing happened. He did it again.

"I'm not sure it's getting into her," he said.

I put my arm under her knees and back and lifted her. She was a bag of bones. She was skinnier than the last time I saw her. She probably hadn't eaten since.

Backdoor," I said. Boyce got to the squad car before me and opened the door. Holding Reggie like a baby, I slid in. Boyce came in beside me. The cops were in the front seat and we were rolling before Boyce got the door shut.

I held Reggie tight. I could feel the sharp angle of her shoulder blade, and her ribs were like those of a skeleton. She smelled sour, like old discarded meat.

"Come on, baby," I said. "You can make it. We're almost there."

The cop in the passenger seat was on the radio, talking to the hospital. Boyce had hunched around and was watching us. She reached out and put a hand on Reggie's back, gently rubbing her. Then I felt inexplicable tears running down my cheeks. "Hold on, baby, hold on," I crooned to her. I had seen my share of death. I'd had friends and colleagues die. I had put a tourniquet on the shattered leg of one of my first teammates and watched him bleed out before help could arrive. What made this little drugged up loser any different? I turned my head, so Boyce couldn't see. But, she was watching.

The patrol car came roaring into the hospital drive, screeching to a halt under the Emergency Room overhang. They were waiting. They tore my door open and pulled Reggie from my arms They put her on a gurney and were moving inside before I could get all the way out of the patrol car.

The Emergency Room was familiar. I had been in it when they were digging a slug, meant for me, out of Boyce's beautiful body.

I stood there, looking around, not sure what to do. They had hustled Reggie off, through the swinging doors and out of sight. I felt Boyce come up beside me. I turned to look at her. Her eyes were wide and compassionate as they searched my face. She put her hand on my arm.

"Out of our hands now," she said.

I shook my head, slowly. "The Naloxone was running down her face. It never made it in her."

"Maybe some of it."

I shrugged, and shook my head. Hopeless and helpless. Two of the worst things ever.

"You staying here?" she asked softly.

I nodded. "Yeah. Right now, I'm all she's got."

"I need to get some sleep," she said. "Mendoza's got me shadowing the supplier tomorrow, so I have to be up early."

"Like you say. Out of our hands. You go get some rest."

She stepped into me and hugged me. She held on longer than a normal goodbye would take. Finally, she broke away and turned, and without looking back walked out the automatic door. The two cops followed her.

The waiting room was mostly empty with one Hispanic family. The mother was trying to comfort a crying baby. I found a corner and tried to rest, but couldn't. I found magazines and tried to read, but couldn't. Finally, I stretched my feet out, leaned back, and closed my eyes. All I could see was Reggie's pale little face shining up at me from the dark.

I must have dozed off. Someone sat in the chair next to me. This was an emergency room faux pas. You didn't sit directly next to someone unless there were just no seats left. I opened my eyes.

"Sorry Jackson," Father Correa said. "I didn't mean to wake you."

"Just resting my eyes, Father," I said. I sat up and tried to unkink my shoulders. "Why are you here? One of your girl's in trouble?"

"Detective Boyce called me. She thought you might want

some company. And, yes. One of my girls is in trouble."

I smiled. I have to admit, I was glad to see him.

"Father, it's three o'clock in the morning," I said.

He smiled back. "God's work isn't on a time clock. Have you heard anything."

"No, afraid not. And, that's not a good sign. We tried the heroin antidote, but I don't think enough got into her."

"The spray?"

I nodded.

He reached over and patted my hand in sympathy. He looked at me, "Jackson, would you mind if I pray?"

"Right now, I'll take all the help I can get. But, you know me, Father. I'm not much of a prayer."

"Everyone prays, Jackson. It is just that we don't all do it the same way. The world is a wide and diverse place, and prayer is just as diverse." He laid a hand on top of mine. "Some of us make a conscious act of it. Closing our eyes, getting on our knees. Saying our prayers as a direct and conscious act. Now I lay me down to sleep….Some of us, and I believe this includes you, pray in a way that you don't formally call it a prayer. But, I believe it is prayer never the less."

I frowned.

"Let me explain," he continued, patting my hand. "Have you ever found yourself sitting alone, relaxed, in the quiet, maybe in the dark, and your mind is searching for something? Maybe a solution, maybe just clarity. But, some form of understanding. And sometimes, you find the understanding and sometimes you don't. But, your heart and your mind are receptive to finding it. Have you ever had that experience?"

I nodded.

"That, in my opinion, is praying. To me, that is God allowing you to use the gifts he has given you to gain deeper understandings. If you hear a voice of understanding, it may be God's voice, or it may be your own, but he is the one that granted you the grace to hear it. So, like I say, I think everyone prays. Some people just don't use that word."

"Pray away, Father."

He lowered his head. I watched him. "Lord, we bring to you our friend Reggie. She is in trouble and is in need of your help. We know that you are a God that can do wonderous things, and you are a God that allows terrible things. Please place the grace in our hearts to accept, with peace and love, which ever you decide. Bring our little girl the peace she needs, and if you decide to leave her with us on this temporal plane, please give Jackson and myself the strength to help and guide her to become whole again. If you decide it is her time to go, give us the grace and understanding to have peace with that decision."

Instead of an 'amen', he squeezed my hand.

A doctor came through the automatic doors that Reggie had disappeared through an hour earlier. He looked around, and I stood up. Father Correa stood next to me.

The doctor walked over to us, stripping the gloves from his hands.

"I'm sorry," he said, shaking his head. "We did all we could."

44

This time the mountain came to Muhammad. The houseboat wasn't getting much use lately, so I was airing it out. I had the stern and aft sliding doors open, allowing a cross breeze through the main cabin. The air had a lake smell, and I realized I had been missing it. It was a cloudy day and the sun moved in and out of sight. My phone vibrated. I had a text. It was from Boyce. It said *Stay there*.

Why could something so innocuous irritate the crap out of me? It was typical Boyce. Not *are you home?* Not, *I'm coming to visit*.

I went to the bow and looked down the dock toward the hill that led up to the parking. The shuttle was coming down, toward me. The new kid was driving. Boyce was beside him. There was someone in the back, but I couldn't see the face because of the cart's canopy.

Finally, the cart came to a halt at the bottom, and the passengers stepped out. I started grinning. The mountain had come to Muhammad. Captain Mendoza followed Boyce out onto my dock. I looked back inside the boat. I must be becoming domesticated, because I was thinking I should have straightened up. I pushed that foolish thought out of my head and stood on the bow waiting. Boyce was in her Detective outfit. Tan jacket over white, long-sleeved blouse. Badge on her belt. Dark slacks that hugged her hips but were looser on her leg. Mendoza was buttoned down as usual. For some reason, against the backdrop of all these boats, he looked like an undertaker.

They reached me, and Mendoza said, "We need to talk."

"Up top," I said. I stepped back as they stepped on board. Boyce led the way to the top. I snagged three bottles of beer as I went through the galley. I popped the tops, then joined them topside. I handed each a beer.

"This isn't a social call," Mendoza said.

I pulled the canvas covers off of three chaise lounges, and shifted them around in a semi-circle. "No reason to waste a beer," I said. Boyce was already drinking hers.

"Have a seat," I said.

They sat. Boyce was between us.

"Good job with that microphone, everything was crystal clear. Where did you put it?"

"In a bottle of Mr. Boston. My only fear now is that when one of the regulars steals it like they steal bottles of booze every time Frank isn't watching, they'll get it in their windpipe and strangle on a thousand-dollar piece of electronics."

Boyce laughed. Mendoza almost smiled.

"Well, it picked up everything very clearly. Unfortunately, it didn't pick up a thing we can use."

"You had Mr. Stein there. They were talking about selling stolen opioid pills on the streets."

"Yes, and we could make a case about conspiracy, but we already have more than that on Paz."

"Then what the hell am I doing?"

Mendoza reached into his suit jacket pocket and pulled out a letter sized paper folded in half. He handed it to me.

"I haven't been completely forthcoming," he said. "I'm not really after Paz. We could have him anytime we wanted." He looked at Boyce, she was watching me. He looked back to see me looking at Boyce. "Detective Boyce really hasn't been watching Paz, she's been watching for someone else."

"Stein." It wasn't a question.

He nodded. "Mr. Stein's real name is Sherman Kaplan. He is the financial officer for Cyntose Pharmaceutical. A Fortune Five-Hundred drug distributor. Him, and his board of directors are among the big fish we are looking for." He nodded at the paper in my hand. "That's a transcript of the meeting you bugged. You tell me if you read anything there that could bring an indictment against Mr. Kaplan?"

I read it. He was right. There wasn't.

He continued, "Some time ago the DOJ warned us that some manufacturers and pharmaceutical companies were distributing opioids on a larger scale, not just to pharmacies, clinics and doctors, but to street dealers involved with organized crime. We could take down the dealers, but that would be like cutting off a limb and leaving the tree. I don't have to tell you the money those companies have for lawyers. Without a smoking gun, prosecution could drag on for years. They came to me and asked who the logical contact for organized crime in Phoenix was? Paz was the likely connection. We had already been watching Paz for a long time. We just couldn't get anyone inside."

"Until now," Boyce said.

"Until now," Mendoza nodded. "And now we have identified Kaplan. What we need is the smoking gun. Irrefutable proof of Cyntose's complicity."

"How," I asked.

"That's your job," Boyce said.

I just looked at her. "Really?"

"I'm afraid the Detective is right," Mendoza said. "You're the one inside. You know these guys, and they trust you."

I leaned back and looked across the lake. A speed boat was ripping across the water, a thirty-foot plume rising behind him. He was a quarter mile away, but the noise was still obnoxious. I drank the rest of my beer.

"Well, crap," I said.

45

I had set up the next meeting with Tommy four days from my last one. His idea. He said he needed a few days to round up the money. So, I was on the boat, cleaning. I was essentially killing time until it was time to drive south and meet the jerk at the club. I was swabbing down the galley when I felt the bump that made the boat rock. It had come from the aft. I peered down the hallway, and out the back door. I saw Old Eddie's head bobbing up and down. He was tying off his fishing dinghy. I got a beer from the locker and popped it for him.

I stepped out as he was struggling up the back ladder.

"It would be easier tying off on the dock," I said.

"Fuck the dock," he said, pulling his skinny frame up onto the Tiger Lily.

He swung his leg over the back transom, and as soon as he got his balance I handed him the beer. He took a long, grateful swallow.

"Ain't been home much," he said, with a small belch.

"Still working on that Cicero Paz thing," I said.

"Well, looks like you still have your top-knot."

I smiled, "Come on in and set a spell." I moved back inside and he followed. "What brings you to my humble abode?"

"Ain't nothing humble about it. Especially compared to mine. Now, maybe compared to Pete's it may be humble. I'm told the catfish are in the shallows at the north end, and goin' crazy on Bowkers and shrimp."

"Bowkers?"

He pulled himself up on a stool at the galley counter, I sat on the big yellow couch. "I don't believe I've heard of that."

"Stink bait. Hard to come by now days. You stick a frozen shrimp on a number two hook and dip it in the jar of Bowkers and the catfish eat it up. But, mind you, you need to use a dipping stick to shove the shrimp down in the stuff. You don't want to get it on you. You do that, and you won't have relations with a woman for a while. At least not the women you'd want to have relations with."

"So that's what I must have done."

He grinned at me.

"Did you get new teeth?"

"Just two," he said, grinning wide to expose his teeth. "What they call implants. They had a free clinic at the mall, and I went down to check it out. The next thing I know, they're sticking two new teeth in my head. My God, Jackson. I can eat corn on the cob now."

"Allahu akbar!"

"What?"

"Arabic for God is great. Or, in some translations God is greater."

"Ain't that what them terrorists say when they're whacking someone's head off?"

"Yeah, some ass wipes say it before they do something terrible. Stupid to think God is on their side when they do things like that. But it's really just words saying that God is great. A lot of dumb people think it is only used by terrorists, but hell, if you said it in Chinese or Spanish or Portuguese, or English, it would mean God is great."

He finished his beer and cocked his head at me. "You read too much. Messes with your brain,"

I laughed. "I had the radio on. Today one idiot took a journalist to task for trying to explain the phrase. Claimed that just by using it, it made the reporter a terrorist sympathizer."

"You have to quit listening to that shit. It's like a worm. It gets in your head and ruins you. You need to fish more and listen to the wind. How about joining me?" He set his empty beer bottle on the counter and slid off the stool.

"I would in a heartbeat, but I have to go to Scottsdale and catch a fish of my own."

As I watched him motor away, there was a whole lot in me that wanted to be with him.

Six hours later Nacho and I walked into the club in Scottsdale. It was a little after nine. Ass wipe Tommy was at his usual spot. We made our way over and I sat next to him. Nacho took his usual place against the wall.

The waitress came over, but I waved her away.

I leaned into him, "You got the money?"

He shifted around to look more directly at me. He took a white envelope from his jacket pocket and handed it to me. I opened it and looked inside. Inside was a cashier's check for one hundred thousand dollars. I handed it back.

"My associates only deal in cash," I said.

It was at this moment that the DJ started a big, crashing piece of noise someone considered music. Tommy's face was shocked. "What the hell are you talking about?" he said angrily.

"That document," I explained, pointing at the check, "can be traced back to the bank that issued it, and therefore can be traced back to you. Cash can't be traced."

"You're joking!"

"Do I look like I'm joking?"

"How the hell do I get cash?"

"Not as hard as me getting gold."

He sat back, staring at me. I met his gaze without wavering. We had already figured this out. Our guesses were right.

Finally, he said, "Tomorrow night, same time." He pushed himself up and around the table and stormed out.

I looked at Nacho. He winked at me.

46

Nacho and I walked in the club just about twenty-four hours later. Tommy was waiting. He had a package on his table. The place was noisy and packed. It must not be a school night. Almost everyone there looked like college kids.

I was carrying the .45 caliber Kahr in a shoulder holster. I followed Nacho through the crowd. The kids parted like the Red Sea. I sat next to Tommy and Nacho took his place against the wall. I looked over the room. I waved at the waitress. I saw Tommy's eye flit to the gun under my jacket as it opened slightly as I waved.

The waitress came right over. The way I had been tipping, I was one of her favorite customers. I ordered a Johnnie Blue. I pointed at Tommy's untouched drink, "Get him another." He didn't protest.

I nodded at the box. "That it?"

He slid it to me. "Want to count it?"

"You bet your ass I'll count it, but not in here. You are too smart to stiff me. If it's short, you're done. I sure as hell won't give it to my guys short. That's a fast way to a bullet in the brain."

"Open the box," he said.

I waited for the waitress to deliver the drinks. When she moved away, I slid the top of the box open. Inside were neat stacks of hundred-dollar bills. I dug down deep, and pulled out a stack from near the bottom. I slid one bill out and studied it. I held it toward the light, looking for the water-mark imprint of Benjamin Franklin that would verify its authenticity. It was there. I placed the bill back in the stack and the stack back in the box. I closed the lid.

"I had a helluva time with the bank, getting those," He said. He took a drink. "

"I can imagine. But, that's the way it has to be."

He nodded. He understood. He'd have done the same thing. "The goddam manager had to cover his ass and call his boss, and the boss was tied up, so I ended up waiting for over an hour, so they could clear the bills."

"It'll be worth it," I said.

"How long you think, before we get the gold?"

I sat back, more relaxed now that I saw he had the money. "This isn't going to be overnight. Keep in mind the gold is mostly dust and you have to sift tons of tailings to get any at all. That Pete guy was lucky he got so much so fast."

"I'm having seconds thoughts," he said.

"Second thoughts?"

"Yeah. I don't even know how to get in touch with you. You could just walk out with the money, and poof!"

I was nodding. "Yeah, that's true. But, you didn't just think of that. If you want your money back, here it is." I touched the box. He was looking at me, making up his mind.

He put a hand on the box, "I want to see the operation in action. I want you to take me to it, so I can see it work, then you get the money."

I grinned at him. "What? You don't trust me?"

"Hell no, I don't trust you. I've got just about every penny I could get together in that box. If you are scamming me, I'll shoot you myself." He pulled his jacket back to expose, what looked like a Glock in a shoulder holster.

"Don't worry," I laughed. "You're going to be rich."

"Well, let's go then."

Nacho came over to us and said, "Heads up."

I looked at him, and he was looking toward the door. Coming in the door was Blackhawk and Pete, with Boyce bringing up the rear. Blackhawk and Pete were wearing cheap suits with a badge pinned to the lapel. Boyce had a crisp white blouse with her holstered pistol and her badge on her belt for all to see. She also sported a blond wig that made her look like a Dolly Parton action doll.

"Shit!" I exclaimed. Tommy swung around to look.

"Hey, that's…"

"The asshole's a cop, I've been had," I said. I looked at Nacho, "Get him out of here," I said.

Nacho grabbed Tommy by the arm and pulled him up, "Come on, we gotta go."

"What the hell?" Tommy said.

"Out the back way," I shouted.

Blackhawk had spotted us and they were making their way through the crowd, shoving those that didn't move fast enough. Nacho began dragging Tommy toward the back hall which led to an emergency fire door. I stood and slowly raised my hands. Blackhawk had a revolver in his hand. Pete had taken his badge from his lapel and was waving it around like he meant business. His other hand was on the handle of the empty Glock he had holstered on his belt. The box of money was on the table.

"You are under arrest," Blackhawk shouted above the din, at the same time Nacho pushed Tommy through the emergency door, and the emergency lights began strobing. A shrill siren cut through the air. This was my clue. I grabbed the box of money and bolted toward the door. People were yelling as I slammed into them in my desperate attempt to escape. My waitress dropped a tray of drinks and fell backward. Boyce was yelling at me to stop. Pete was waving his badge around, and Blackhawk started after me.

I made it to the door, and burst out into the artificial light of the front parking area. I began to sprint across the lot. Blackhawk burst out behind me, followed by the rest of the posse. He was yelling for me to stop. I glanced over my shoulder, and caught a glimpse of Nacho and Tommy at the back corner of the building. Tommy had stopped to watch.

Blackhawk took a stance and began shooting. On the third shot I pitched forward, skidding on the asphalt, the box sliding ahead of me with packets of money spilling. Men and women had come bursting out behind Boyce, and some of the women screamed.

Blackhawk, Pete and Boyce surrounded me. Pete picked up the money. Boyce knelt down beside me and appeared to check my pulse. What she really did was pinch my cheek. She's hilarious.

She looked up and said in a loud voice, "He's dead."

I lay there, sprawled out, while they stood around me. More and more people were gathering. A couple of slow minutes passed, then Nacho pulled his Jeep into the parking lot. He maneuvered it to beside me. He rolled his window down.

"All clear," he said, out the window. "I brought him around to the side and he saw the shooting, and heard Detective Boyce. Then the little fucker shoved me away, and ran like the wind to his car. He burned rubber all the way down the block." He was laughing.

I stood up, brushed off my pants and the front of my jacket, and climbed into the Jeep. Pete handed me the box though the window. Nacho drove us away. In the mirror I watched Blackhawk, Pete and Boyce walk over to Boyce's car. She had left it by the front entrance with the lights flashing. Red and blue splashes of light raced across the front of the building. They all climbed in, and she cut the lights and drove them away. A small bewildered crowd gathered. Trying to figure out what the hell had just happened.

Nacho glanced over at me. He was grinning, "Slick, Dude. Just fucking slick."

47

The next night, in the wee hours, I met Boyce downtown at the station. I carried a satchel with fifty thousand dollars in it. Half of Tommy's ill-gotten bucks. She was at her desk, waiting. I took the elevator up, walked down the hall and into the large squad room. Toward the back, Mendoza's office was dark. Only one other detective was there. He glanced my way, then went back to his newspaper. Boyce had her feet crossed on her desk, her hands locked behind her head. She watched me walk across the room before she sat up. There was no smile of greeting.

I sat the satchel on her desk. She didn't look at it.

"You know," she said. "Before I met you I don't think, at the most, I had broken two laws in my life. And speeding was one of them."

"Was murder the other," I said. I pulled a chair and sat.

"No," she said. "But, since I met you, I think about it a lot."

Now she looked at the satchel. She pulled it to her and snapped it open. She peered inside. She sat back and glanced

246

at the detective across the room. He was absorbed in world events. She looked at me.

"I need to record these serial numbers," I said. "I'm going to get this money in Kaplan's hands then you and Mendoza can put him in the slammer."

Boyce looked at me a long time. I recognized this look. She wasn't looking at me, she was thinking. The detective across the room stood and tossed his paper aside. He slung his jacket across his shoulder and started by us.

"Hey Boyce," he said. "Be sure to turn off the lights. I don't want Mendoza on my ass."

Boyce gave him a thumbs up.

She said to me, "We have an oversized copier downstairs. We can lay these out and scan them. We'll have a record." She was thinking again. She took a memory stick from her desk drawer and slid it into her pocket.

"I think I have a way to get this in his hands," I said. "When Kaplan has it, I'll let you know."

She stood. She took the satchel. "It's downstairs. We'll take the stairs." She started across the room. I followed.

The stairwell stank of old, used up, human despair. It made you realize how old the building was. Boyce went down the stairs rapidly. With my foot, I wasn't as agile, so I ended up a few steps behind when she finally came to the landing she wanted. She pushed through the door. I caught it before it slammed me in the face. We went down a long hallway. We made several turns before she came to double doors. She went through, snapping on the lights. The room was filled with filing cabinets. At one end was a cage that filled that end of the large room. The cage had to be part of their evidence storage. There was a chest high window in the mesh where goods could be dispersed or received.

Against one wall was a wide, oversized copier. Next to it, a utility table. The kind you can fold the legs up inside the underneath. The kind of table every church in the world has stored in their basement.

Boyce lay the satchel on the table and unloaded the packages of one hundred-dollar bills. She carefully unwrapped a bundle, lifted the copier lid, and began laying them, face down, on the glass of the copier. She fiddled with the controls. I could see on the LED screen, it was set to scan. She took the memory stick from her pocket and slid it into a USB port on the side of the copier. She hit the start button and after some clicking and whirring, the copier scanned the first batch of bills.

"Blackhawk says those things are obsolete," I said.

"What? The copier?"

"Those little memory stick thingies."

"Everything in this building is obsolete," she said. "Okay, your job is to bundle up the bills after they are scanned. I'll lay out a new batch." I started gathering up the bills while she unwrapped another one. It took over an hour, but eventually all the bills were back in the satchel.

Boyce was studying her fingers. "I have to wash my hands," she said. "God knows what was on those bills."

"Mostly cocaine," I said.

She looked at me. "When Kaplan has the cash, you'll call me."

"That's what I said," I said.

She turned and flipped the lights out. We left. I waited until I reached the boat before I washed my hands. Actually, I washed my whole body.

48

It was 3:30 in the morning. The streets were dead. Blackhawk jimmied the back door to the SanDunes, and we went in. We were both dressed in black, with black watch caps and rubber soled shoes. We each carried a backpack. We also each had a holstered Glock 17, 9mm strapped to our thigh. I had brought the guns from the storage unit I kept under a false name. The storage unit was packed with stuff. Stuff that had been important in my past life.

The back room was cluttered with bar junk. Old bar stools, old beer signs, boxes of glassware and cleaning supplies. It smelled dusty and musty. I knew there had to be rats here. To my knowledge, it had never been cleaned. I also knew the room was windowless, so I snapped on the pencil light I had carried in my pocket. Out of habit I had taped the lens with black electrical tape, leaving the tiniest of openings. The light was just a thin strand, but it illuminated everything we needed to see. We silently opened the inner door on the other side of the room. We stepped out into the hallway that ran from the bar to Paz's office. Paz's office door was on our left. Of course, it was locked.

Blackhawk knelt down in front of the lock, his zippered case of strange tools open in front of him. I held the light.

"Don't leave any marks," I said.

He stopped what he was doing and turned to look up at me. He held my eyes for a long second. I shrugged. He shook his head in disgust and bent back to the task. He had it open in under thirty seconds.

Paz was a bad guy. If he felt inclined, he would cut your feet off and feed them to the carp in the Encanto Park Lagoon. He had been the top bad guy for a long time. It caused a certain arrogance. He just couldn't believe someone would mess with him, so he didn't take great pains to hide stuff. Someone a little less confident would have sensors and sirens and infrared do dahs all over the place. Not Paz.

His safe was built into the wall behind his desk. He must not have watched any old movies. He didn't even have a hinged painting in front to hide it. It was just there for all to see.

I stood to one side and held the light on the dial. Blackhawk pulled a stethoscope from his backpack. Yeah, I know, this sounds old movie corny, but it works.

"How many?" I asked.

He held up three fingers. He believed there were three tumblers, the wheels inside that spin to the proper number to release the lock. Most cheap locks have three number combinations. He took out a small notebook and a pencil. He wrote a number on it. He hooked on the stethoscope and with one slender hand held the sensor next to the dial, and with the other, slowly turned the dial, listening intensely.

There is a small rod, sometimes called a *fence,* resting gently atop the wheels. It is attached to a lever mechanism that keeps the safe locked. As long as the fence is in place the safe remains locked. Each wheel has a notch, or a *gate*, at one point along its circumference. The trick is to rotate each wheel to get all three notches at the top, so the fence falls into the notches. Like a log falling into a trough. Then the handle on the door will move and the door will unlock.

As Blackhawk gently rotated the dial, he was listening for a click. The click was when the gate bangs into the *lever*, the stationary part attached to the fence. Bangs may be a little strong, but there would be a click. He would note the number on the dial, then go the other way. Sometimes it was several tries. Sometimes it was the adjacent number, so it wasn't an automatic. But, Blackhawk was the best I'd ever seen.

He meticulously moved the dial back and forth until he was satisfied. He had several numbers noted on his pad. He marked through all but three and handed the note pad to me. I handed him the flashlight, spun the dial several times clockwise, then to the first number, back past the first number to the second number, then back clockwise to the third. I pulled the lever and the door swung open.

This was the critical part. If the safe was empty, my plan was screwed.

It was full of cash. Of course it was. Paz dealt in cash. There was no way he wouldn't have at least a hundred G's on hand. We were incredibly lucky. Paz's cash was wrapped in the standard bank strips, very similar to the cash in my backpack, so we didn't have to do a lot of shuffling. I pulled Paz's cash out and laid it on his desk. Blackhawk counted it. One hundred ten thousand and fifty dollars. Fifty dollars? What the hell? Was that going to be a tip for someone? Blackhawk spread our cash out. The bundles of Paz's that had been in front, the most visible in the safe, I placed on top of my cash. Now, again, there would be one hundred ten thousand and fifty bucks in the safe. Fifty thousand in hundreds with serial numbers on Boyce's memory stick. I placed the front layer of Paz's cash, backed by our cash in the safe. Blackhawk stuffed the fifty thousand of Paz's cash into the backpack.

Blackhawk closed the safe and spun the dial several times. He then moved the dial back to the very first number he had written down. It was the number the dial had been resting on at the beginning. He never missed the smallest detail.

He handed me the flashlight. I moved the beam around the room, looking for anything that we had moved out of place. We were good. We went back out into the hallway, into the storage room, and out the back.

Boyce was sitting beside the dumpsters, waiting for us. She was a dark lump, illuminated by the one back light that hadn't failed yet. I could see she wore a full, ratty looking, bag lady dress that was long enough to cover her knees to her feet. She had a really nasty looking sweater she had found somewhere and she had a black stocking cap on. She sat against the wall, with her elbows on her knees, smoking a cigarette.

The cigarette glowed as she took a drag. "You boys find what we need?" she said. She stood up and stumbled, catching her heel on the hem of the dress.

"Careful, now," Blackhawk said.

She flicked the cigarette out into the parking lot. It caused a shower of embers.

"Why don't you just send up a flare," I said.

She had lifted the hem of the dress and was looking at it. "I can't remember the last time I wore a dress this long," she said. She looked at me, ignoring my comment. "Did you get it done?"

"Yeah, we got it done."

"So now what."

"I'll let you know," I said with that exasperated feeling I usually get with Boyce.

"Hey, guess what," she said brightly, turning to Blackhawk.

"What," he said. He had a lot more patience. But then, he had been with Elena a long time. That was a PhD in patience.

"The other day I got bored, so I decided to follow Peggy for a couple of days. Want to know what I found?"

"For Christ sakes, Boyce," I said. "Can't you just tell us what you have to tell us?"

Blackhawk was smiling, "What?" he said.

"Peggy has a lover. Can you believe it? Who'd a thought it."

Even I was surprised by this. "Peggy?" I said.

"Wanna know who it is?" She looked like the cat that ate the canary.

"I can hardly wait," I said.

"I followed him to a bar down on Seventh, called Rosie's."

Blackhawk started laughing.

"What's so funny," I said.

"Rosie's is a gay bar," Blackhawk said, still laughing.

"Peggy's gay," I was incredulous.

"Guess who he met there," Boyce said, smiling.

"For God's sakes, Boyce," I said.

"I'm not joking," Boyce said. "I couldn't believe it. I sat there for two and a half hours until they came back out. I watched them kiss in the parking lot."

"So, who was it? Some downtown boy toy hooker?"

"It was Pony Boy."

Yikes.

49

Little Joe crooked his finger at me, and I followed him into Paz's office. Wally Chen, Peggy and Vanilla were already there. Paz was behind the desk. I moved to an empty spot on the wall and leaned against it. The wall safe was staring at me like I was an old friend. I winked at it. Sitting on the floor next to it was a piece of carry-on luggage. The kind with the wheels and retractable handle.

"We've got our people in place. They get a thousand pills apiece," Paz said without preliminaries. "They sell them for thirty bucks. Every other day we collect the money and count the pills they have left." I did the math in my head. He had at least twenty dealers. That's thirty thousand a pop, if they sell out. That's $600,000 every two days.

"What if they sell them for more than that?" Vanilla asked.

Paz shrugged. "Hell, I don't care, they can keep the extra. We collect $30 bucks a pill. It'll make the math easier. They make back ten percent. We pay them on the spot." He looked hard at us. "It's your job to keep them honest."

I didn't smile.

"Anyone shorting us gets a broken finger. If it happens twice, we take care of them."

"Do we have the stuff?" Peggy asked.

Paz shook his head. "Stein says they will have it at the Scottsdale clinic. Little Joe, you and Wally pick it up this afternoon. Twenty thousand pills. Stein says it's a starter package, to see how we do."

"His name's Kaplan," I said.

Paz looked at me. It wasn't a friendly look. The rest looked at me too.

"How do you know that?" Paz said.

"It's not rocket science, Boss. Once I knew the name of the clinics, which wasn't hard to find out, I got on the internet and found the mother company, Cyntose. I searched their HR files, and I found him. Had a nice picture. He's the Comptroller. The guy that was with him is Walter Tillburg. He's a security specialist working for Cyntose."

Paz leaned back in his chair, studying me. Wally Chen was drilling me with his impenetrable dark eyes. Little Joe was looking at me, a small frown on his face.

"You run very close to being too cute," Paz said.

I shrugged, "Look at it from my point of view. If I'm caught with a few thousand hillbilly heroin pills, and a bunch of hundred-dollar bills in my car, I'm looking at twenty years. I don't take that kind of risk unless I'm sure I'm good."

"Hillbilly heroin?" Wally Chen said. Paz was thinking.

Finally, he said, "So, you go with Little Joe and Wally."

"I've been thinking about that."

Paz leaned forward and put his hands, palms down, on his desk. "Oh, please enlighten us."

"When Kaplan came here, he shook us down. He didn't want to be recorded."

"So?"

"If we go to pick up the stuff, do you think a clinic like Cyntose might have surveillance cameras everywhere."

"He's right, boss," Little Joe said.

"So, they have the goods on us, but they are free and clear. We're a bunch of assholes stealing the stuff from their warehouse. Kaplan has the video that means we get twenty years hard time. At least for whoever picks the stuff up. If the cops turn one of us, then you join us at Florence. Kaplan holds all the cards."

Paz was nodding.

"I'd never do that, boss," Little Joe said.

"The hell you wouldn't," Paz said, without looking at him. "Trade twenty years to be State's evidence. Hell yes, you would. Anyone would."

He looked at me, "Okay, smart guy. How do we do it?"

"He needs you. You are the only game in town. Pike can't do it alone, but you can. What we need is détente. We need leverage on Kaplan, like he has on us."

"What the hell is détente," Peggy said.

"Equal threat," Wally Chen said.

"Mexican stand-off," Little Joe said.

I nodded. "He has something on us. We have something on him. Nobody gets hinky without putting himself in jail."

"So how do we do that?"

"You tell Kaplan he has to meet us, himself, at the loading dock. Or wherever we're supposed to pick the stuff up. He has to hand it to us personally. We record it. Wally can record it on his phone. Now we can feel safe."

"Why me?" Wally Chen said.

"Because everyone knows you chinks are electronic whiz's," Peggy smiled.

Even Paz smiled. Wally Chen didn't.

"What makes you think he'll go for it?" Paz said.

"Because you will insist. You tell him you won't play without insurance. It's called poker. He can't win the pot unless he puts money in the middle, and you have the only poker game in town."

Paz thought about it. Finally, he said, "Give me the room."

We all went back out into the bar to wait. Frank set up beers for us. A few minutes later Paz came out.

He looked at me, "It really pissed Kaplan off," he said.

"But, he will do it," I said.

He smiled, "You're a smart little shit. Yeah, he'll do it. You, Little Joe, Wally and me at two o'clock."

"You're going, Boss?" Little Joe said.

"Yeah, I'm going. The prick acts like he thinks he's in charge. He needs to know he ain't."

So, at one thirty, we drove out of the SanDunes parking lot. Little Joe drove, I sat in the passenger seat with Wally Chen in back with Paz. Paz had placed the small, rolling carry-on in the trunk. The distribution clinic was called

Adobe Mountain Pain Clinic. It was in a high rent retail center east of the 101 Loop and Frank Lloyd Wright Boulevard in Scottsdale. We pulled into the complex parking lot at two.

"Go to the back, where they take the shipments," Paz said.

"You think he'll show?" Little Joe said.

"He better. If he doesn't, we just fucked a sweet opportunity," Paz said sourly.

Little Joe wheeled the car through the shoppers and around the parked cars to the end of the complex. It was a long complex, with all the retail spaces connected so that the back was one long, connected wall broken up only by rolling metal doors and loading docks.

As we drove around to the back Little Joe looked at me, a question on his face.

"It was the fourth one," I said. He nodded. He maneuvered the big car around some semis and pulled in next to the fourth loading dock. There was a small plaque reading *Adobe Mountain Pain Clinic* attached to the wall next to the rolling metal door.

"Got your camera?" Paz said to Wally Chen.

"I have my phone," Wally Chen said.

"Whatever," Paz said. "Just take the video."

Paz pulled his phone and hit a number. He waited a second. When it was answered, he said, "We're here." He disconnected and climbed out. I went out my side. Little Joe cut the motor and hit the trunk release, then stepped out. I glanced at Wally Chen. He had taken his phone from his back pocket and was fiddling with it. I noticed Little Joe took his pistol out of his shoulder holster and put it in his belt.

Paz pulled the carry-on from the trunk. We stood there long enough for me to begin to doubt. But, greed won. The smaller door opened, and Walter Tillburg stepped out. Kaplan was right behind. Paz carried the bag up the concrete steps and Kaplan shook his hand. That was a good sign.

"I don't see why this is necessary," I could hear Kaplan say.

"Think about it," Paz said. "It'll come to you. Have you got the stuff?"

Kaplan looked at Tillburg. Tillburg stepped back into the building and brought out a large cardboard box. Little Joe looked at me and cocked his head toward Paz and Kaplan. I went up the concrete stairs two at a time, and took the box. It was heavier than I expected. It was taped shut. I set it down. With my pocketknife I slit the tape and opened it. It was stuffed to the top with gallon baggies of pills. I held one up, and held it out to show Paz, but really to make sure Wally Chen could get a good shot of it. While I did this, Kaplan unzipped the bag. I was happy. He picked out a bundle of bills, looked at it, front and back, and replaced it. I put the baggie back, and carried the box to the car. I put the box inside the open trunk.

I heard Kaplan say, "Don't expect this to happen every time."

"I don't," Paz said. "But it needed to happen this time." He came down the steps and climbed into the back seat.

Little Joe slid into the driver's seat. I opened my door and stood watching as Kaplan disappeared inside. Wally got in behind me. I heard Paz's door shut. Tillburg stood watching me.

"This could be the beginning of a beautiful friendship," I said in my best Bogart. I shot Tillburg with my forefinger and thumb and slid into the passenger's seat. Little Joe backed and filled and drove away.

Back at the boarding house, I called Boyce.

50

Paz had the pills counted and bagged. A thousand pills filled a zip-lock baggie to the brim. The next afternoon, as I sat at the bar, Little Joe came up to me. He was carrying a satchel.

"Paz wants you to come with me," he said. He moved on past without waiting.

I slid off the stool and followed him out. We took his BMW. It was really a nice car. Not a Mustang but nice.

"We making a delivery?" I asked.

He nodded. "Three of them." He glanced over at me as he maneuvered through traffic, "You sure came at the right time. This is going to be a gold mine."

I stifled a smile. I already had one gold mine thing going.

"So, you guys already have dealers lined up?"

"Oh yeah, Paz's been at this a long time. Before him was Manny Munro. Dealers ain't hard to come by. Most of them are addicts. They sell to afford their own stuff." He glanced at me, "They don't bite the hand that feeds them. They do, they lose the hand. And, worse for them, they lose their supply."

"They'll make a lot of money too."

"Oh, yeah. They don't know it yet but they're going to be very happy. Once the word hits the street that you can get your opioids at your neighborhood corner dope dealer. Oh, man!"

"Think they can move a thousand pills in a day or two?"

"Once the word is out we'll need more than that. We sell at 30 bucks a pill. Somebody's gonna get smart and start buying at $30 and start selling at $40. Like the boss said, this is a trial run."

"Who buys at $40?"

"Addicts are everywhere. Say you are someplace remote. If you can't get it at $30, you'll pay $40. A smart guy buys five hundred pills at $30. You drive to the Verde Valley, you sell at $40, you make five grand for a day trip."

"Ain't free enterprise a good thing," I said.

The first stop was at a small dark bar on Seventh Street called Paddy O'Briens. Walk in the door and you are in 95% of the neighborhood bars in America. If you were blind and deaf, the smell alone would tell you that. I followed Little Joe's massive shoulders through the door. He carried the satchel. It was mild outside, so the door was open and the inside somewhat illuminated. The bartender looked at Little Joe then nodded toward the back of the room.

Seated at a back booth was a skinny guy in a red ball cap and dirty tee shirt. He was reading a newspaper, the pages folded back to the racing pages. Little Joe slid into the booth opposite him. I stood. The guy lowered the paper. He looked a little shocked.

"You guys already collected," he said.

"Not here for that," Little Joe said. He sat the satchel on the table and opened it. He pulled a baggie of pills out and sat them in front of the guy.

"There's 500 oxycodone pills in here. They are all yours"

The guy shook his head, "I didn't buy no oxycodone."

"Didn't say you did," Little Joe said. "It's a gift from Cicero Paz."

The man's eyes widened.

"He just wants you to sell them."

"Sell them?"

"Thirty dollars apiece. I'll be back tomorrow night and collect for what you've sold. You get ten percent." Now he had the man's attention. "You do good, we'll get you even more."

The man looked at the baggy like a dog looks at a steak. "These real?"

"They're real," Little Joe said.

The man opened the baggy and took a pill out. He put it in his mouth.

"You owe us thirty bucks," Little Joe said sliding out of the booth.

51

I was stretched out on the bed at the boarding house, fingers locked behind my head, wondering how I was going to tell Mrs. Haggerty I would be moving. When I had come in, Mrs. Haggerty and Mrs. Eberle had their heads together at the dining room table. I only heard a few words before they heard me and stopped talking. Mrs. Eberle was saying, "He should have called me by now." Her tone was one of worried anxiety.

Now, my phone was on the dresser, and it began to vibrate. I rolled off the bed and picked it up.

"I'm two minutes away," Blackhawk said and disconnected. Not two and a half minutes. Not one minute fifty seconds. Two minutes.

I went to the closet and selected a fresh shirt. I slipped it on, sat on the bed and attached my foot, then slipped on my shoes. They were white New Balance's. They were made by a specialty shop on Bell Road, just to accommodate my prosthetic foot.

At the top of the stairs I heard Blackhawk's voice below.

It was two minutes. I came down. Mrs. Haggarty and Mrs. Eberle were in the living room. Blackhawk was seated on the old brocaded divan. Next to him was an expensive looking briefcase. A business card was on the coffee table. Mrs. Haggarty was offering him tea.

"Thank you, Ma'am," Blackhawk said. "That would be wonderful."

With a smile, Mrs. Haggerty hustled to the kitchen, Mrs. Eberle looked up and spotted me coming down the stairs. "Oh, Jack," she exclaimed. "Come join us. This is Mr. Black from the bank."

Blackhawk stood, and I shook his hand, "Pleased to meet you, Mr. Black," I said.

"Likewise," he said. We both sat.

Mrs. Haggerty stuck her head around the corner, "Would you care for some tea, Jack?"

"Certainly," I said.

I looked at Blackhawk, "What brings you our way, Mr. Black?"

He cleared his throat, "Well, to be frank, my business here is with Mrs. Eberle." He looked at her, "It is of a personal matter."

"Is this about my husband Elmer's account?"

Blackhawk frowned, "I thought his name was Elwood?"

"Well, that was his given name," Mrs. Eberle said. "But he hated it. He was born with the name Elwood Merle Eberle, but he changed it to Elmer."

Mrs. Haggerty came in with a tray of tea service. She sat it on the coffee table, in front of Blackhawk.

"Do you take sugar or milk, Mr. Black," she asked.

"No thank you Ma'am. Plain tea is fine."

She poured a cup and set it on a saucer in front of him. She set a dainty napkin next to it. "How about you, Jack? Sugar or milk?"

"Both," I said.

She placed a sugar cube in a cup, poured milk from a small matching pitcher, and then poured the tea. She delicately set it in front of me. She poured a cup for Mrs. Eberle, then herself.

Once settled, she said to Mrs. Eberle, "Is this about Elmer's money?"

Mrs. Eberle said to Blackhawk, "Mr. Black, anything you need to say, you can say in front of Mildred and Jack. They have my complete trust."

Blackhawk looked at both of us. "Very well, then," he said. He shifted to seem a little uncomfortable. "I am from the fraud department of the bank. It is my job to investigate whenever the bank feels that someone is trying to defraud the bank. Or, in this case, one of the bank's customers."

Mrs. Eberle looked distressed. "The young man assured me everything we were doing was on the up and up. I never had any intention of doing anything wrong." She looked at Mrs. Haggerty. "After all, it was my money. Or, at first Elmer's, but he is deceased. I felt I had a right to it."

Blackhawk held his hand up. "I'm not here to cause you a problem, Mrs. Eberle. What was the name of the man that came to visit you, saying he was from the bank?"

"He wasn't from the bank?" exclaimed Mrs. Haggerty.

"No, Ma'am, he wasn't."

"He had a business card," Mrs. Eberle said. "Just like yours." She picked up Blackhawks card and studied it. "Just like this one."

"What was his name?" Blackhawk repeated.

"Edward Burns. He said he saw me at the bank. Why was he at the bank if he didn't work there?"

"The only Edward Burns employed by the bank is in Oklahoma," Blackhawk said. "The man that came here to your house was named Grover Hilland. What did he tell you?"

"Well," she glanced at Mrs. Haggerty, "he said that he heard my name at the bank, and he was researching old abandoned accounts. And, one of those had the same last name. But, it was in the Elwood Merle name, not Elmer, so that's why I never knew of it." She flushed slightly, "Mr. Eberle liked to gamble. Mostly on the horses. He spent a lot of time at Turf Paradise. So, he must have put his winnings in an account with Elwood instead of Elmer."

"And, Mr. Hilland said he had a way for you to get it?"

"He said his name was Mr. Burns," she said emphatically. "He said it could all get wrapped up in red tape. And I didn't have a way to prove that my Elmer and Elwood were the same person. I don't have a birth certificate or anything."

"She's telling you the truth," Mrs. Haggerty said.

"Yes, Ma'am," Blackhawk said. "I'm sure she is." He placed his elbows on his knees and tented his hands. He looked very reflective. Academy award stuff.

After a long moment, he said, "How much did the man

269

say was in the abandoned account?"

"Forty thousand dollars."

"Did you think about consulting an attorney?"

She looked like she was about to cry, "No."

"How much money did you give him?"

"I gave him my CD."

"How much was that?"

"Thirty thousand."

"And, you haven't heard from him since?"

Now she was crying. Mrs. Haggerty came over and put her arms around her, making little cooing noises. I gave Blackhawk a look.

"I have good news and bad news, Mrs. Eberle."

Mrs. Eberle snuffled. "What does that mean."

"The bad news," he continued, "is that your husband never had another bank account in the name of Elwood, or Elmer."

"But, that man said he did."

"The good news," Blackhawk continued as he set the briefcase on his knees and snapped it open, "is that we caught up with Mr. Hilland before he got away, and we retrieved your thirty thousand dollars."

Mrs. Haggerty's hands flew to her face, "Oh, my goodness! Oh, my goodness!"

"Oh, my," Mrs. Eberle exclaimed. "Is it true? Is it true?"

"Yes, it's true," Blackhawk said. He pulled the packets of one hundred dollar bills out of the briefcase and stacked them on the coffee table. The last thing he pulled from the briefcase was a pink deposit slip.

"I highly recommend that as soon as possible, you fill out this deposit slip, and take the money to your branch and deposit it."

"Can't you do that?" Mrs. Haggerty said.

Blackhawk and I just looked at each other.

Blackhawk stood. "No, Ma'am," he said. "Trusting strangers is what got you into trouble in the first place. I have to catch a flight back to the home office. Perhaps, Mr. huh, Jack can give you a lift to the bank. I wouldn't delay."

"Happy to," I said.

"So pleased to meet you ladies," Blackhawk said. He squeezed both of their hands, and shook hands with me.

"So long now," he said. He went out the screen door, careful not to let it slam.

Mrs. Eberle was dabbing at her tears with one of the delicate napkins. "Oh, Mildred, can you believe it? What a nice young man," she said.

"Yes, he was," Mrs. Haggerty said. "It is just wonderful." She looked at me, "But Jack, didn't you think his hair was a little long for a banker? I guess the world is changing."

52

I was sitting at my usual stool at El Patron nursing a Dos Equis. Across the rectangular bar from me Elena was deep in quiet conversation with her friend Anita. Anita had come in a few minutes ago sporting a new shiner. Her left eye had a distinctive, puffy, mouse under it which had resulted from a smack administered by her right-handed husband. As Anita snuffled into a napkin, Elena was leaned into her, their heads just inches apart. I couldn't hear the words, but the tone was fierce. I wouldn't want to be that poor sap.

Blackhawk came down the stairs and slid up on the stool next to me. When Anita had come in, Nacho had found something to do at the other end of the bar. Likewise, Jimmy was cleaning glassware feverishly, down there with him.

Blackhawk wiggled a finger at Jimmy and Jimmy brought him a club soda with lime, then hustled back to the other end.

I was watching Elena. "So, do you think Elena will have the poor simple bastard killed, or just drawn and quartered."

"I think drawing and quartering would probably kill

him. But, I don't think she'll have him killed. Probably more an eye for an eye." He took a sip. "Maybe castration, but I doubt Anita would like that. Fate is a fickle thing. Just think. That ignorant bastard is probably sitting in a bar somewhere, happy as a lord, unaware of his own impending doom."

"Happy as a lord?"

"I'm feeling especially poetic today."

"What will she do?"

Blackhawk turned the glass in his hands. "Elena has many friends. She'll have one of them do her a favor."

"Not you?"

"Oh no, not me. She saves me for heavy work."

"Like her cousin, Diaz?"

"Boyce took care of that for me."

"Yes, she did." I noticed Nacho looking past me, toward the door. I swiveled on my stool.

"Speak of the devil," I said. Boyce was coming down the hallway, through the open door into the bar. She spotted Elena and Anita and detoured to them. Elena gave her a hug and I could tell, was explaining the situation, but again, her voice was too low to hear. Boyce was patting Anita on the back.

"I could take him downtown," Boyce said. This I heard.

Anita immediately shook her head and began to cry harder. Boyce stood there for a moment, patting Anita on the back. She looked over at me. She walked around the bar and sat next to Blackhawk. She was watching Elena and Anita.

Jimmy came up to her, "Get you something, Detective?"

Boyce looked at Blackhawk's drink. "What's that?"

"Club soda and lime," Blackhawk said.

"Get me one of those," she said to Jimmy. "What's she going to do? You think Elena is going to have the bastard castrated?"

Blackhawk laughed. I had to smile. "I think, in the long run, Anita wouldn't want that," Blackhawk said.

Jimmy sat Boyce's drink in front of her.

"This a social call?" I said.

"Do you want it to be?"

"Why do you always have to answer a question with a question?"

"Why do you have to know."

"If you two are going to go on like this, I'm going back upstairs," Blackhawk said.

Boyce laughed. "I thought you might like to hear about your boy Grover-Edward-Tommy."

"What about him?"

Nacho and Jimmy must have heard her, they both moved closer.

"Captain Mendoza was very taken with my tale about the boy. He was especially interested in where you got a bag of gold." She cocked her head at me. "You didn't tell me that you had gone to the Captain for a bag of gold."

I shrugged, "I thought maybe there was an off chance he might have something like that in the evidence room."

"A bag of gold?" she said.

"It was worth a shot."

"You didn't even tell me where you got it."

"You didn't need to know."

"Where did you get it?"

"You still don't need to know. What about Tommy the grifter?"

"You're not going to tell me, are you, you prick."

"Tell me about Tommy."

"Tell me where you got the gold."

"Tell me about Tommy first."

She was glaring at me. She's really cute when she's mad. She took a drink of the club soda and took a deep breath. "After I told Mendoza the whole story, or at least the parts I knew," she gave me a look. "Mendoza put a young, college-looking detective into the club under cover. He watched Tommy pick up a young girl and leave with her. Tommy followed the girl to an apartment over by ASU. The Detective ran the girl's plates and learned the car was registered in a man's name. The Detective got the information on the man and called him. It was the girl's father." She leaned back and looked at me.

"That's not the end of the story," I said.

"Guess what the father told the Detective?"

She could exasperate me. "I don't know. That a full moon makes your hair fall out."

"The girl was underage," Blackhawk said.

"Oh, shit!" Nacho said.

Boyce was smiling, "You got it. So, the Detective called for a patrol back up and they went in and busted the guy for soliciting a minor for sex. Caught them in bed."

"So, that guy is up shit creek," Nacho grinned.

Boyce finished her club soda and set the empty on the bar. "So, where did you get the gold?"

"I'll tell you sometime," I said.

She slid off the stool, angry. "Fuck you, Jackson. You are such a douche." She stormed away.

"He got it from Emil," Blackhawk called after her.

"Bucket mouth," I said.

"You need to be careful," Nacho said to me. "That girl carries a gun."

For the first time I noticed that Elena and Anita were watching from across the bar. They must have heard the whole thing.'

"What gold?" Elena said, standing up. "And, who's this Tommy guy?"

"See what you've done," Blackhawk said to me. "I'll be upstairs."

53

Paz was in a celebratory mood. The first shipment of pills had sold out, his dealers were ecstatic and begging for more. It was like opening night for a blockbuster film. He had Frank chase all the regulars out of the bar, then demanded that Frank set up champagne for all. The problem was, Frank didn't have any. So, he sent me out to buy some. In the meantime, Frank started pouring shots. I went outside and walked across the parking lot to my car. The air was cool and there was a distant hum of traffic from a few blocks away. Before I got into the Mustang I stretched my arms out and took deep breaths of the cool air. I looked around. It was dark, and I saw nothing. I knew we were being watched. I could feel Boyce out there, somewhere. Luckily, there was a Fry's market close by. I bought ten bottles of Brut there. That was all they had.

Frank had me uncork all the bottles. He said the sudden explosion of the corks unnerved him. Frank handed out all the white wine glasses he had, and poured a generous helping of the bubbly to each of us. All of Paz's and Pike's guys were there. Even some dealers with their women. Vanilla was there. Everyone was in the party mood. Pony Boy and Peggy were standing at the middle of the bar. Both, holding shots, leaned back, elbows against the bar, looking cool. I couldn't help but watch them. Tough guys in love.

Paz held his glass high.

"Quiet down," Little Joe shouted. He raised his glass.

We all quieted down, raising our glass with his.

"This is just the beginning," Paz said. "Tomorrow we pick up a shit load of these little golden pills, and we are going to sell every one of them. I don't have to remind you that we will be counting every pill that goes out, and every dollar that comes in. At the end of the week, I'll get a count on what you sold and you all will get a really sweet paycheck. In the meantime, let's tie one on!"

They all cheered. Wally Chen was smiling, he didn't cheer. Smiling for him was jumping up and down in ecstasy. Also, I noted, he was the only one that poured more champagne. Everyone else went back to the hard stuff. Frank was busy. One of Paz's bigger dealers was in my regular stool, so I sat on an empty just one from Pony Boy and Peggy. Little Joe went to the jukebox and studied it for a long time. Finally, he fed it coins, and it began blaring the Beatles *Eight Days a Week*.

I heard Pony Boy say to Peggy, "That's what we'll all be working if those guys have their way."

Those guys were Paz and Pike, who were sitting at the end of the bar. Both were smoking cigars, with a rock glass of amber liquid. They were in intense conversation. No doubt counting money they planned to make.

At the end of the song, and before another one could begin, the door opened. And, there she was in all her glory.

I thought, *Oh, shit.*

Bag lady Boyce walked in. Ratty watch cap, filthy sweater, holes in improbable places. Long ragged dress. And, even though I couldn't see them, I knew her shoes were a pair she had found in a dump.

Everyone in the place turned to look. I turned also. I could watch the rest of the room in the mirror. Peggy slid off his stool and moved by me. He stood in front of Boyce, but she tried to move around him. I had no idea what she was trying to prove. Peggy grabbed her arm. The crowd went quiet.

"Let go of me, you fuckin' fag," she said loudly.

Peggy was shocked, "What did you say?"

She tried to yank away but he held her tight.

"Hey, Pony Boy, why don't you get your lover boy off of me?"

I swung around. Paz and Pike were both staring.

Peggy swore. "You goddammed bitch," he said and shoved her hard. She stumbled backwards. She caught her heel on the hem of the dress and fell hard, rolling up on her shoulders. Her legs were flailing in the air, her dress up around her waist. I moved off my stool and got between Peggy and Boyce just as he was trying to kick her. She was quick, and scrambled back.

I grabbed Peggy's arm, "Calm down," I said. "Calm down, I'll get rid of her."

He tried to shake my arm off, "Let me go, you son of a bitch!"

I tried to leverage him sideways, but he was one giant muscle. Boyce scrambled to her feet, her back against the door. Peggy started swinging at me. Big, roundhouse swings. I covered up, and tried to get out of range, but I had no room and was up against the bar. I did my best rope a dope but one of his swings slammed through my arm and hit the side of my head. The bells were ringing. He kept swinging. He had no finesse, just brute force. My shoulders and upper arms were taking a beating. Everyone had scrambled away. I managed to get a stool between us and tried holding him off like a lion tamer. He threw another hard, wide right at me and I got the stool up enough, and he hit the metal leg with his knuckles.

He howled and stepped back looking at his fist. I dropped the stool and leveraged my right foot against the bar. As I pushed off, I hit him with everything I had. I caught him on the jaw. Now, I think we both had a busted knuckle. He staggered back but didn't go down. I ignored the pain in my hand and rapidly hit him twice more. He fell back against a table, and I kicked him in the chest with my prosthetic. He went down. Little Joe stepped between us, holding his hands up.

"That's enough," he shouted. Peggy was trying to get up. Little Joe shoved him back down, "That's enough," he said again. He didn't have to convince me.

He looked at me, "Get her the hell out of here. Make sure she doesn't come back."

I backed away, then turned to Boyce. She was still against the door. I grabbed her by her sweater and yanked her, so I could get the door opened. The sweater tore, but I managed to hustle her outside. In case someone was watching I hustled her across the parking lot. She was grinning.

"He's a big sumbitch, ain't he?"

"What the hell do you think you're doing?" I gave her a small shove.

"Mendoza's sending SWAT," she said. "The DA has sworn out warrants on Kaplan and that whole bunch. Now it's Paz's turn. I want those assholes to know who it is that's going to arrest them."

"Peggy could have killed you."

"But he didn't. Besides, isn't that what Mendoza wanted you to do? Protect me?"

I just shook my head. "Not if you are committing suicide."

She laughed and moved off into the shadows.

I stood a moment, then slowly walked back to the door. I took the handle, hesitated, took a breath, got Jack back in my head and went in.

Peggy was up and sitting on a chair. The fight was out of him. He looked at me as I came in, but I saw no rage. Just the same old Peggy. Paz was standing by him.

"What the hell did she mean?" Paz was saying, "About you and Pony Boy?"

"I have no idea," Peggy said.

Paz turned to Pony Boy, "Are you guys queer?"

Pony Boy looked at Pike, then back to Paz.

"It ain't none of your goddammed business," he said.

"I got queers on my team?" Paz said, incredulously.

Peggy was rubbing his jaw, where I had hit him. Pony Boy turned his back on Paz, and lifted his drink and drained it. Little Joe stood, looking from Paz to Peggy, to Pony Boy and back to Paz.

I heard the door open and I thought here comes the cavalry. I turned.

Bernie and her young cowboy, Butch, came stumbling in. They were so drunk they could hardly stand.

"Hey, you fuckers, it's time to party," Bernie yelled. "Me and Butch are getting married! Set'm up Frank."

I think we were all stunned.

They came falling in, holding on to each other, barely able to stand. Giggling as they moved into the room. Bernie got to the stool where she normally sat, which luckily was empty, and pulled herself up. She looked around. "What the hell is going on here?" she said. "Somebody havin' a birthday?"

The door opened again.

It was Boyce.

She had changed out of her bag lady clothes, and this time it was Detective Boyce. She had her shield in her hand. Holding it up for all to see. She took two steps into the room and was followed by the SWAT team.

There was a commotion from the back, and now the back hall was filled with SWAT. They had come in from the storeroom. It became pandemonium.

"Listen up, you assholes," Boyce shouted above the

screams. "You have the right to remain silent. Anything you say can and will be used against you in a court of law. You have the right to an attorney. If you don't have an attorney, one will be provided for you. Do you understand your rights?" She didn't wait for a reply. She turned to the SWAT team. "Boys, you can bet every one of these assholes are carrying. And, you can bet your sweet ass they are dangerous. Please disarm them."

Looking out the open door into the parking lot I could see two wagons, lights flashing, waiting to take Paz and the rest of us downtown. The SWAT team swarmed us, pushing us against the bar. Some of the women screamed. Paz couldn't believe it. His head swiveled from side to side. Little Joe had his hands up. Peggy and Pony Boy stood shoulder to shoulder, but did nothing. Wally Chen remained seated until a cop grabbed him by the arm and pulled him up. They began to frisk us. Slowly, one by one, they started shoving people through the door, to the trucks.

Bernie and Butch were loudly protesting their innocence. I think Butch was too drunk to understand what was happening. As they were shoved toward the door, Bernie pointed at Frank, who was still frozen behind the bar, and shouted, "This does it Frank, I ain't never coming here no more!"

As the cop walked Wally Chen toward the door, Boyce stopped them. She put one hand on Chen's lapel and with the other, reached inside his jacket. She pulled his phone out. She fiddled with it a moment, then smiled. Wally was watching her, then turned to look at me. I turned my back as a SWAT guy shoved Little Joe and me up against the bar. He searched us. Little Joe had a pistol in his shoulder holster, and he had an ankle gun. The guy pulled my .38 from my back pocket. He herded us out. As we went through the door Little Joe said, "I knew she was a cop."

I had to laugh. I looked over my shoulder at him, "You knew she was a cop? Bullshit. How long did you know she was a cop?"

"Since Peggy knocked her down. Hell, ain't no bag lady in the world has panties that white."

54

The air was still and warm, hot even. Two days ago I had gassed up the Tiger Lily, emptied the honey pot, and stocked the locker with fresh vegetables, prime beef and good wine. The bar was stocked, and the ice coolers were full. We were way up north on the lake. I had chugged up past South Barker Island and up the Aqua Fria river. This area was normally closed off to protect the eagle population that nested up here. However, it was open this time of year. I liked coming up here because the local boating enthusiasts were so used to the area being closed, there was little traffic.

Blackhawk had helped me place the two bow anchors, and the stern anchor. You drop the stern anchor first, then letting a lot of line out, move up to where you want to drop the bow anchors. I usually drop the bow anchors forty to fifty feet apart. Once they are solid, you position the boat between them and back up until the lines are snug. Then you haul in the stern line until it is tight, leaving just enough slack to prevent the wind from lifting the anchor off the bottom. It doesn't hurt to swing a little. If you've done it correctly you won't awaken the next morning to find yourself banging against the bank.

Quite unexpectedly, just after daybreak this morning, Old Eddie had come alongside and dropped off some two-pound catfish fillets onto the bow. The sound of the motor had pulled me out of sleep, but by the time I had strapped on a foot, and stepped through the sliding doors to see him, he was already moving away. He raised an arm in salute. I waved back.

Fresh caught catfish. Yum. I had washed them, wrapped them in paper and put them in the locker to stay cool. We would feast tonight. I already had a really tasty fish rub, some corn on the cob and a cornbread mix. I knew I would have a battle with Elena, she had never eaten catfish. But, I knew that as soon as she had a bite, she would be sold.

Detective Boyce had taken some accrued vacation days, and Blackhawk and Elena had left Nacho and Jimmy in charge of the bar. The four of us were on the upper deck, on chaise lounges, next to the iced cooler of beer. Boyce had gotten into the hard apple beers. Elena had a Corona and Blackhawk and I had Dos Equis. We were lathered in SPF 50 sunscreen and about as lazy as people can get.

Elena had plugged a mini-speaker into her phone and had downloaded some Mexican music. I didn't understand a word the singers were singing, but the music was quite pleasant. It made the day even more festive.

Boyce finished her beer and got up and tossed her empty into the recycle tub. She pulled another from the cooler and popped it with the church key I had tied to the cooler handle. She looked at the rest of us, but no one was ready. She had on a yellow bikini. She was pink from two days of sun. I admired the puckered little dot in her flesh that never would tan like the rest. This was where she was hit by the bullet intended for me.

She came back and sat beside me.

"I got a text this morning from Mendoza," she said.

"Oh?"

"The Grand Jury indicted Kaplan, that Tillburg guy, and most of Cyntose Pharmaceutical's board of directors. And, the management of that pain clinic. They offered Kaplan a plea deal and he's singing like a canary. Putting the finger on the manufacturers that supply him. This thing could go national."

"What about Paz and Pike?"

"They indicted Paz, Wally Chen, Peggy and Vanilla of drug dealing charges."

"Not Little Joe?"

"He didn't mention Little Joe."

"What about Pike and Pony Boy?"

She took a drink of her apple beer and looked at me. She had that smile on.

"What," I asked.

"Pike cut a deal," she said.

"With the prosecutor?"

"With Mendoza."

"What kind of deal?"

"Without Paz, and without Pike, someone else will move in to fill the vacuum. I guess Mendoza didn't want to start all over, so he decided to leave Pike in place. Where he can be controlled."

"Isn't that illegal?" I smiled. "In collusion with a drug dealer?"

"Says the ex-government assassin," she said, taking a drink.

"You don't know that."

"I know a lot more than you think."

"Well, you can't prove it."

"Would you guys stop. I'm getting hot," Elena said. "Let's go swimming."

She stood and placed the mostly empty bottle next to her chaise lounge. She went to the side of the boat and looked back at Blackhawk, "You comin'?"

He stood, "Sure."

She reached behind her back and unsnapped the top of the two piece. She let it drop to the ground. Sliding her thumbs into her bottoms, she slid them down and stepped out of them. This was one magnificent view. She dived into the water below.

"That just ain't fair," Boyce said.

Blackhawk went to the side and slid his trunks down. He dived.

"Tell me about it," I said.

"Oh well," Boyce said. She stood and moved to the edge of the boat. "If you can't lick'm, join'm." She unsnapped her top and slid out of the bottoms. She did a cannonball, landing with a huge splash.

I stood at the edge of the top deck looking at the three of

them. Naked as eggs, treading water.

"Come on Jackson," Elena yelled. "The water is good."

"Don't be a chicken," Boyce called. Then she started making chicken noises.

I was shaking my head.

"Come on, buddy," Blackhawk called. "Don't leave me down here with these two women."

"Oh, what the hell," I said out loud. I hooked my thumbs into my trunks, and down they went. I teetered on the edge, then as I pushed off, my good foot slipped. I hit with a really bad belly flop.

THE END

Following is an excerpt from
number four in the acclaimed Jackson Blackhawk series.

Coming Soon

THEY CALLED HER INDIGO

by Sam Lee Jackson

The girl was white blond, her hair in a short cut that swept across her forehead. She was quite beautiful in a young pixie kind of way. She was very good. She waited until my machine hit, then when she put her hands into my clothes I didn't feel a thing. But I knew she did it. The only thing I noticeably felt was the absence of my wallet as she turned to move away. I waited a moment before I glanced at her. I swiveled on my stool and looked the other way at Blackhawk. He was three slot machines down watching, a smile on his face. I shrugged, cashed out of the machine, pulled my card and slid off my stool. He followed suit.

He went the long way around two lines of slot machines, all the while keeping her in sight. I followed more directly, staying well back. She didn't target any more guys, but wound through the crowd to the back, where a bank of elevators awaited.

We were at one of the Indian tribe casino's that populate the Phoenix area. I never could figure out the law that said Native Americans could own gambling establishments, but other races couldn't. I'm sure there was some kind of reason, but since I don't gamble, it wasn't something I stayed up nights worrying about.

Blackhawk had made a friend that managed this particular casino. The guy had become a regular at El Patron, Blackhawk's night club, and a big fan of Blackhawk's girl Elena with her big salsa band. The guy was always trying to persuade Elena to come perform at his casino, but she was happy where she was. He and Blackhawk had been engaged in idle conversation over a cocktail, when he mentioned that he felt the casino slots were being cheated. He couldn't figure out how. Blackhawk said he would look into it, and invited me to tag along while he checked it out. So, here we were, playing quarter slots, with me getting my pocket picked.

The girl was a pro. A very young pro, but a pro. She knew where the cameras were, and she knew too many stops behind unsuspecting men would bring security down on her. I stayed back while Blackhawk followed her onto the elevator. I noted every floor the elevator stopped at. When it came back down, I followed an older couple on. They gave me a harsh look when I pressed the button for each of the previous stops. One of the stops must have been theirs, they didn't attempt to press another button. They got off at the first stop. Blackhawk was waiting at the second.

"End of the hall," he said. Without waiting, he turned and started down the hall. I followed. I could have grabbed the girl as soon as she took the wallet, but this is how Blackhawk and I have our fun.

He reached the door, and moved to the side, his back against the wall. Just out of sight of the peep hole. I knocked. After a moment the light in the peep hole darkened. Someone was looking at me. I put on a nice smile and knocked again.

Whoever was looking at me, hesitated. Then I heard voices. I couldn't make out the words, but the tone was inquisitive. The door hesitantly opened. It wasn't the blondie, but another young girl of about the same age. She had brown hair, and a fading bruise on her cheek bone.

"Yes?" she said.

"Hi there," I said brightly. "I'm here to pick up my wallet."

She started to shut the door abruptly, but I had my foot in it. I shoved it open, which shoved her back. I stepped into the room. Blackhawk stepped in behind me. The blond was sitting in a chair, where she had been looking through my wallet, but it was the woman on the couch that had both mine, and Blackhawk's attention.

The woman was tall and slender, wearing tight jeans, and an embroidered blouse. She sat casually, her legs crossed with a tooled boot on each foot. Her hair was blond, but not as white blond as blondie. Fashionable streaks highlighted her hair in an expensive looking way. She held a throw pillow on her lap. Her left arm lounged across the top of the couch, the right hand under the pillow.

She began to laugh. "Well, look what the cat drug in," she said.

"They called her Indigo," Blackhawk said in his best deep, movie trailer voice.

"Let me guess," I said. "9mm Beretta?"

She laughed again, taking her right hand from under the pillow. In it was a 9mm Beretta. "Good memory."

Blondie was looking from us to her, "You guys know each other?"

"Long, long ago, in a land far, far away," I said.

"You still go by Indigo?" Blackhawk said.

She placed the pistol on the lamp table beside her. "I told these girls my name is Jane."

"Jane isn't your real name?" the brown-haired girl said.

"Neither is Indigo," Indigo said.

This was when I realized that Blackhawk and I knew this woman better than the two girls she shared the suite with.

She stood and moved to a desk that had been set up as a bar.

"What are you boys drinking?" she said. She looked at me, "I don't have Boodles, just Tanqueray," she said.

"Good memory," I said.

"Tanqueray and tonic," Blackhawk said.

"Make it two," I said.

"Make it three," Blondie said.

"Make it four," the other girl said.

"You girls old enough to drink?" I said.

"Fuck you, Jack," Blondie said.

"Not Jack. Jackson," Indigo said as she fixed the drinks. "His name is Jackson. The tall, dark, handsome one is Blackhawk."

The brown-haired girl snorted. "Blackhawk?"

"His real name is Fred," I said. "Fred Littlewanger."

Indigo handed us all a drink. "You two are still on the comedy circuit, I see," she said. She looked at the girls, "There isn't any little wanger to it. Take my word for it."

My eyebrows went up. "Oh, really?"

"We shared a latrine a long time ago," Blackhawk said. He raised his glass to the two girls, "Blackhawk will do. At your service."

"So, what are you now?" I asked Indigo. "Let me guess, you are Fagan and this is your merry band of Artful Dodgers."

"First of all," she indicated Blondie with her glass, "this is Simone, and this," she indicated the other girl, "is Nikki. I'm just trying to help them out of a little jam."

"What kind of jam," I asked.

Blondie Simone took a drink, and looking at it, made a face. "We have a bunch of people that are looking for us."

"They're going to kill us for sure," Nikki said.

"A bunch?" I said, looking at Indigo. "What constitutes a bunch?"

"By definition, more than twelve," Blackhawk said.

"A bunch," Indigo said. She wasn't joking.

Did you enjoy The Bag Lady, the Boat Bum and the West Side King?

The most important reward for an author is to have his or her books reviewed. If you enjoyed the book, go to the Amazon address below and let us know what you think. After you get there, just click on the book you read, then click on the reviews.

Go to this address to leave a review or for more Jackson Blackhawk reading adventures

Amazon.com/author/samleejackson

Or

www.samleejackson.com